D0249983

FROM
THE DEAD

NORAH McCLINTOCK

FROM THE DEAD

ORCA BOOK PUBLISHERS

Library and Archives Canada Cataloguing in Publication

McClintock, Norah, author
From the dead / Norah McClintock.
(The seven sequels)

Issued in print and electronic formats.
ISBN 978-1-4598-0537-8 (pbk.).—ISBN 978-1-4598-0538-5 (pdf).—
ISBN 978-1-4598-0539-2 (epub)

I. Title.
PS8575.C62F76 2014   jc813'.54   C2014-901545-3
C2014-901546-1

First published in the United States, 2014
Library of Congress Control Number: 2014935394

Summary: Rennie finds out more than he ever wanted to know about his grandfather's
past when he investigates Nazi war criminals in Argentina and Detroit.

*Orca Book Publishers is dedicated to preserving the environment and has
printed this book on Forest Stewardship Council® certified paper.*

Orca Book Publishers gratefully acknowledges the support for its publishing
programs provided by the following agencies: the Government of Canada
through the Canada Book Fund and the Canada Council for the Arts,
and the Province of British Columbia through the BC Arts Council
and the Book Publishing Tax Credit.

Design by Chantal Gabriell
Cover photography by Getty Images, iStock, Dreamstime and CG Textures

ORCA BOOK PUBLISHERS
PO Box 5626, Stn. B
Victoria, BC Canada
V8R 6S4

ORCA BOOK PUBLISHERS
PO Box 468
Custer, WA USA
98240-0468

www.orcabook.com
Printed and bound in Canada.

17 16 15 14 • 4 3 2 1

To A.O. and B.R., for the gift of time.

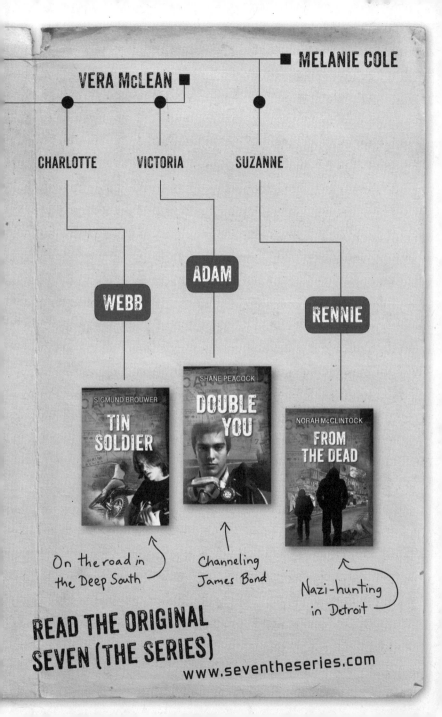

MELANIE COLE

VERA McLEAN

CHARLOTTE   VICTORIA   SUZANNE

ADAM

WEBB

RENNIE

SIGMUND BROUWER

TIN SOLDIER

SHANE PEACOCK

DOUBLE YOU

NORAH McCLINTOCK

FROM THE DEAD

On the road in the Deep South

Channeling James Bond

Nazi-hunting in Detroit

READ THE ORIGINAL SEVEN (THE SERIES)

www.seventheseries.com

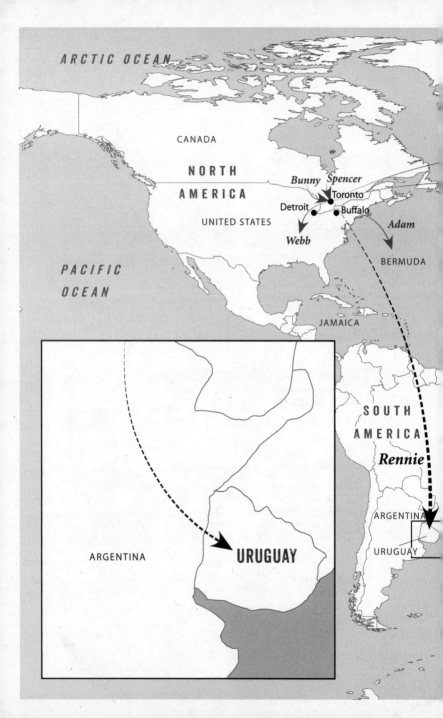

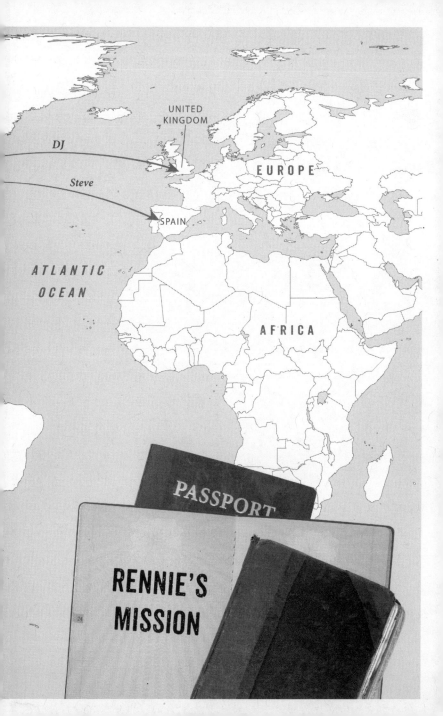

ONE

If anyone had told me I'd be standing, by choice, ankle-deep in snow and ice in a crummy neighborhood in Detroit four nights after Christmas, I would have said they were crazy. First of all, I don't know a single person in Detroit. Second, who in their right mind would choose Detroit as a destination, especially in winter? Third, who would choose to land in a neighborhood that, as far as I can see—which isn't far because there are no streetlights—is on the downward slope to oblivion? Finally, who in his right mind would choose to subject himself to cold, dreary, depressed Detroit because of something that happened half a century ago and that no one—well, *almost* no one—remembered or even cared about?

But here I am, and it's all my cousin Adam's fault. I'll get to that.

Right now I'm standing across the street from *the* house—the one I have the address for, the one that may (or may not) be the key to this whole thing. An old man and a dog are shuffling around a corner out of sight. I'm shivering in my jacket and a marked-down red-and-white Santa-type tuque that ordinarily would make me feel as conspicuous as an alligator in a wading pool. But the house I'm looking at, two stories, paint peeling off its clapboard siding, porch sagging, wooden steps barely visible beneath snow and ice, is the only lit-up place on the whole block. That's because it's also the only non-abandoned, non-condemned place on the block. It's weird. I'm in the heart of a city. If this was Vancouver or Toronto, there would be houses on either side of the one I'm looking at, and houses next to them too, all the way down the block and around the corner. Same thing across the street. That's what you expect in an urban neighborhood. But where I am right now is what *used* to be an urban neighborhood.

The sidewalks are still here, although I bet they're all cracked and broken under the thick layer of hard-packed snow, which no one has bothered to clear. The lampposts are still standing, but, as I said, the lights aren't on. Most of the fixtures don't even have bulbs in them. Intact bulbs, I mean. There's a fire hydrant halfway down the block. I see its top peeking out of a heap of snow. There's also a big metal container that looks like a mailbox, but it's lying on its side and has been kicked so many times that there's hardly a flat surface left. The only way I can see any of this is because there's a clear sky overhead, and without the usual ambient light of a big city, a zillion stars are visible, along with a wedge of moon.

Since I'm here, I decide to get on with it. Nothing ventured, nothing gained, right? I cross the street and climb the porch steps, gripping the hand railing so I don't slip and fall. I make it to the top and almost wipe out on an ice patch on my way to the screenless screen door that does nothing to protect the scarred inner door. I feel around for a doorbell but don't find one. So I knock. The sound—sleeve-wrapped knuckles on wood—is muffled, so I slide an already-cold hand out from the protection of my jacket and rap again, harder this time. My knuckles sting from the cold and the contact.

No one answers.

There's a light on. It's the only one, as far as I can tell, and it's right inside the door. But when I go up on tiptoe to peek through the tiny window near the top of the door, all I see are the front hall and a staircase to the second floor. There's no sign of life.

I knock again.

I tell myself no one's home. I tell myself I'll come back tomorrow. But I can't resist shifting to the right to peek in through the living-room window. At first I don't see anything. It's too dark inside. I press my nose against the glass and cup my hands around my eyes. That's when I see it: a body lying on the living-room floor. I'm pretty sure it's a man. In the light from the front hall, I see that he's wearing a robe and pajamas. I also see a walker—one of the ones with wheels and a little basket attached to the front, the kind that old ladies shuffle behind at the mall. This walker is lying on its side, which makes me think its owner—an old man, or maybe a disabled man—fell down and is in trouble. Either that or he's dead.

He's definitely not moving.

I have a cell phone in my pocket. I could take it out and dial 9-1-1. But—don't laugh—I did my homework before I came up here, and I know that it takes an average of thirty minutes to get a response from a 9-1-1 call in this town. It used to be different, but what used to be isn't going to help me now. I wrench open the screen door and twist the handle of the inner door.

It's locked.

So I apply my shoulder to it, you know, as in I throw myself against it, like a cop on a TV show.

Bad idea. If my shoulder could scream, it would wake the neighborhood.

I stumble backward, massaging what will probably turn into a massive bruise. That's strike one, but I'm still at bat. I check out the door. It's as decrepit as the rest of the house. And I happen to be wearing my favorite Docs—lace-ups with heavy soles and heels. So I aim my foot at the area to the immediate left of the door handle and kick it karate style.

The doorframe splinters. The door flies open.

I race inside.

The man on the floor—now that I'm up close, I see that he's as ancient and rundown as the house—is warm to the touch, but I can't tell if he's breathing. I glance around for a light switch but don't see one, and I don't want to waste time looking for one. I press my ear close to the old man's face. I feel a faint breath on my cheek. He's alive.

"Sir? Sir, can you hear me?"

The old guy moans.

I fumble in my pocket for my phone.

The old guy's eyes open.

"Help me up." His voice is weak and wavery.

"Maybe I should call an ambulance," I say. "Maybe you broke something." Another thought occurs to me. "Do you have a heart condition, sir? Do you feel pain anywhere?" Pain is a symptom of a heart attack—isn't it?

"Help me up," he says. He moves to brace his hands on the floor.

"I don't think that's a good—"

He's trying to push himself up, but he's having trouble getting his arms to accept the weight he's putting on them. But does that stop him? No, it does not.

I get to my feet, squat and slide my hands under his armpits, which, it turns out, are moist.

"Ready?"

He nods.

I start to pull him to his feet, thinking it will be easy. In his thick, heavy robe and what I assume are pajamas underneath, he looks kind of bulky. But his bony wrists and ankles and his long, thin face give me the impression that he's all dried out and won't be heavy. Getting him to his feet should be like swinging a little kid up into the air. But it isn't. The old guy is dead weight. I have to try a second time, bracing my legs so I don't strain my back. Up he comes. One of his hands clutches my arm. I'll say one thing for him: he's got a good, strong grip.

"My walker," he says, wheezing.

I help him over to the nearest piece of furniture—a bookshelf—and get him to hang on while I retrieve his walker and set it right-side up. I wheel it over to him, and he grabs hold. He's breathing hard, which makes me worry that he's going to collapse again. But he doesn't. He pushes his walker over to the wall and throws a switch; the room floods with light.

Then, instead of thanking me, he says, "Who the hell are you? What are you doing in my house?"

"I saw you lying on the floor in here. I thought—"

The old man looks at the window. He's scowling when he turns back to me.

"How?" he demands. "How did you see me lying on the floor?"

I'm thinking of the best way to answer when I hear footsteps behind me and the distinctive sound of someone racking a shotgun. A deep voice barks, "Hands up or I'll shoot." He sounds like he means business.

I swallow hard and remember something I overheard on the plane. A man in a business suit was telling his seatmate that in Detroit a person has the right to shoot an intruder in his house. He also said that Detroit accounts for 43 percent of all concealed-weapons permits in Michigan, which means you don't want to get on the wrong side of anyone when you're there because you never know who's packing. He swore there were church ministers in Detroit who carry guns—while they're preaching!

I glance at the doorframe. It's shattered, thanks to me and my Docs. The lock is likely broken. No one invited me in, yet here I am. And that, I believe, fits the definition of intruder in any and every jurisdiction you'd care to mention.

My life doesn't exactly flash before my eyes. But certain parts of it do. Specifically, the part a couple of days ago when I stopped minding my own business—which, I believe, is the best way for anyone to spend his life—and started minding someone else's.

TWO

Three days before my first-ever venture into Detroit, I was finishing up a Christmas-break/pre-embarkation (for the Major, not me) vacation in Uruguay. Montevideo, to be exact. Down there, unlike back home, it was summer, and that meant some serious beach time. In fact, I spent what was supposed to have been one of my last mornings listening to the ocean and staring (gaping? ogling? definitely drooling) at some pretty senoritas in string bikinis that exposed smooth, sleek expanses of suntanned skin and long-baby-long, long legs.

"*Rentres tes yeux dans leurs trous,*" said someone beside me. The Major, dripping saltwater. "*Et ta langue dans ta bouche.*"

Right, as if it was my fault my eyes were bugged out and my tongue was trailing like a parched dog's on a sizzling July afternoon. Put a dozen guys, any guys in the world, old, young, anything but blind, on the sand near the surf in Uruguay and you'd have been tripping over tongues and eyeballs. Even the Major cast an appreciative glance in the direction of those senoritas when he thought I wasn't looking.

"*Allons-y,*" he said. Let's go.

We'd been in Montevideo for ten days, and ever since we'd arrived, the Major had reverted to speaking 100 percent French with me. With his buddy, an old guy named Ed Mitron, he spoke English. With Ed's house staff—yeah, you heard me; old Ed has an entire staff, housekeeper, cook, gardener, chauffeur—he exercised his Spanish and insisted that I exercise mine. Which was no sweat. If you know French, Spanish is a breeze. And when there are girls around like the one I met five days in and spent one entire day with, trust me, you have all the motivation you need to practice your language skills.

The Major was on me the whole time about manners. "*Cet invitation, c'est un honneur. C'est un homme auquel je dois beaucoup. Ce qu'il m'a enseigné a sauvé ma vie. Alors, sois bon. Tu comprends?*"

Yeah, yeah. I'd been hearing that story for weeks: how the Major owed his life to Ed, how if it wasn't for what Ed had taught him, he'd have been dead long ago, and how, as a result, I'd better be on my best behavior. "Or else" wasn't said, but it was strongly implied.

Ed was the one who had invited us down here. He and the Major hadn't seen each other in a long time. How long, I'm not sure. But they must have talked, because Ed was up-to-date on me. He knew I'd been in Iceland. He knew I was there because of my mom's father, David McLean. He asked me a million questions about how things were in Iceland these days (which made me think he'd visited the place at some point in the past) and about what kind of guy would send his grandsons all over the world fulfilling his last requests. I had to tell him I didn't exactly know. The truth was, I'd only met David McLean once in my whole life. The Major knew more about him than I did, and he filled in Ed as best he could.

The Major toweled off as we trudged up the beach to our rental car. Ten minutes later, we were back at Ed's. Ten minutes after that, the Major was packed and dressed and the three of us, the Major, Ed and I, were in Ed's limo, being driven to the airport by Ignacio the chauffeur.

The Major was saying his goodbyes to Ed before joining the line for airport security when my phone vibrated.

It was Adam.

Check your email NOW, his text read. You are NOT going to believe this, but we're all in.

Adam is one of my cousins on my mother's side. There are six of them in all, and I didn't even know they existed until a year ago. Adam and I had stayed in touch after our grandfather died.

"*Alors, mon fils,*" the Major said, "*sois bon pour ta grand-mère.*" As if I was ever anything but good for Grandma—my mom's mom, not the Major's. She's okay for an old lady. In fact, she's better than okay. "*Je te revois dans un mois.*" A month without the Major would be the closest thing to a picnic I could have in January, but, of course, I didn't say that. Instead, I let him engulf me in a massive bear hug.

"*Au revoir, papa*," I said.

Ed and I watched the Major disappear into the security-check lineup. He didn't turn for one last goodbye wave, but then, I didn't expect him to. That wasn't the way the Major operated.

"Well, how do you want to spend your remaining time in Uruguay?" Ed asked. I was due to fly back to Toronto in two days for a visit with my grandma. From there, I would return home to finish my last semester at school. But first I wanted to see what Adam thought was so important. If I'd had the same kind of phone as he did and the money for a decent data plan, I could have hit the Net then and there. But I didn't.

"I have to find an Internet café," I said.

"No, you don't."

"But I need—"

"Rennie, you insult my hospitality. You can use the computer at my house. You can use any of the facilities at my house. There is no need even to ask. After all, how could I refuse anything to the son of the man who saved my life?" That was one thing the

Major forgot to tell me but that old Ed had been going on and on about since we arrived. The Major had pulled Ed out of the line of fire somewhere in Kuwait—they both happened to be there, for different reasons, when Iraq attacked. To listen to the two of them, you'd think all guys ever did in the military was save each other's butts. That and indulge in a whole lot of what Grandma would call male bonding.

And in case you're wondering, yeah, Ed actually talked that way—all Spanish manners, like in the movies. Ed is short for Eduardo. He's a native Argentinian who was educated in the United States and recruited, according to the Major, by people in Washington who knew a good man when they saw one. Recruited for what, he didn't say. The Major operates on a need-to-know basis, which means if there's no life-and-death reason for me to know something, he doesn't tell me. Another thing about the Major—he doesn't go in for hero worship. But he definitely admires Ed Mitron. Seeing the Major with his old mentor was like watching a twelve-year-old girl melt at the sight of her favorite boy band.

Ed is a lot older than the Major, and from what I've been able to figure out from their conversations, they met when Ed was the head of some overseas operation that the Major was involved in. I say "operation" because it's not clear to me—and neither of them chose to explain—exactly what they were doing "over there" or even where "over there" is, or was. Ed was retired now and living the life. He came across like what my grandma would call a gentleman. He was always having your glass filled before it was empty or a snack fixed before you realized you were hungry. And he did his homework. He was as up-to-date on the Major and his career as he was on me, and he didn't hesitate to offer advice. The Major listened, but I don't know if he intended to take any of it.

So after the Major boarded his plane, Ed and I went back to Ed's place, where he ushered me into a massive sun-drenched room facing the ocean. There was a desk in front of a wall of windows, a computer to one side of it, and a printer on a small table.

"Take as much time as you need," he said. "I have some errands. I'll see you at dinner."

I settled into the desk chair and went online. A minute later, I was in my email account and checking what Adam had sent me. His email didn't make any sense! I went back to the top. There were four sections, each with its own attachment. In the section for attachment one, he'd written: You won't believe this, but it's true. This is NOT a doppelganger. AND it's one of a dozen, all with different names.

One of a dozen what?

I clicked on the first attachment. It was a scan of a passport, complete with photo. I recognized the face—I'd seen enough old pictures of it by now—but the name was wrong. I don't mean misspelled. I mean dead wrong. I hit the Print button.

Not a doppelganger. Did that mean what I thought it meant? Was I really looking at a picture of my grandfather—not Grand-père, the Major's dad, but my mom's dad, the guy I didn't even know existed until a year ago? If that was what I was looking at, why did the signature under the photo—and the name printed next to it—identify the passport holder as Klaus Adler? My grandfather's name was David McLean.

Adam said this was one of twelve. Twelve what? Twelve pictures? Or…twelve passports? Is that what he meant? Twelve passports, all with different names? Why would my grandfather have twelve passports and twelve—what? Aliases?

I went back to the email and Adam's note next to attachment two. We also found a notebook. We haven't figured it out yet, but all the pages have little flags drawn on them. We figure the flags match up with the passports.

I clicked on the second attachment. It consisted of four pages from a small notebook with a little flag drawn in the bottom right-hand corner. I didn't recognize it. The pages were filled with neatly printed letters, but they didn't spell any words I know. They must be in some kind of code.

Attachment three: This one's a doozy! I hoped it was the key to the code for attachment two.

It wasn't. But it *was* a doozy.

It was a scan of a brief newspaper article, accompanied by a much larger photo of three men in military uniform. And not just any military uniform, but World War II Nazi uniforms, complete with swastikas. One of the three faces was circled. But why? Who was he? What did he have to do with David McLean?

Attachment four: Somewhere in Argentina? Maybe Buenos Aires? It was also a notebook page, this one with a hand-drawn map on it and what looked like an address scrawled under it. The writing wasn't the same as on the rest of the pages.

I reread the entire email.

My cousins were a jump ahead of me. Five of the six had gotten together at grandfather's cottage the day after Christmas. The sixth was in Spain. They'd been in touch with him. Apparently, they were looking for more firewood and they stumbled on the passports and a bunch of other stuff. There's money, Adam wrote. If I needed some, he could arrange a transfer. The cousins who were at the cottage had come up with a theory and decided to put it to the test. Some of them had taken a passport or two, and whatever information they could find, and were going to try to track down what it was all about. Had David McLean been a spy? If not, why all the false identities? What had he been up to? And why had he hidden this stuff up at his cottage? Why hadn't he just destroyed it? Had he been planning to do something with it?

I thought about what Adam had written. Sure, I guess my grandfather could have been a spy. That was one explanation for all those passports. But was it the only one? Maybe he'd been on the run. Maybe he had more of a past than we or anyone else in the family knew. Maybe he'd been some kind of master criminal who'd finally retired from the life. Stuff like that can happen.

Get real, I told myself. What were the chances?

Sounds crazy, Adam wrote. Boy, he had that right. But we want to get to the bottom of this. I'm in. And since you're already down there...

Oh yeah, that passport he sent me? It identified Klaus Adler as a citizen of Argentina. Guess what's right next door to Argentina? That's right—Uruguay.

You in? was how Adam ended his message.

I hit Reply and wrote: I'm in.

I admit it: my first reaction was that my cousins were victims of some kind of collective delirium. Grandpa McLean a spy? Still, it made more sense than Grandpa McLean as, say, a one-time Nazi who'd fled to Argentina after World War II and then somehow changed his identity again—or many times—before landing in Canada. I mean, there's no way my grandfather was ever a Nazi—was there? He'd fought in the war *against* the Nazis—hadn't he?

One thing was certain: he had a lot of passports, eleven more than a regular person leading a regular life would ever need. And they were all issued under different names.

Like Klaus Adler. Why did he have a German name? And why an Argentinian passport?

The (few) things I know about Argentina: It's a big country. People there speak Spanish. They're wild about the tango. Oh yeah, and there was this one Nazi, a guy named Adolf Eichmann, the evil genius who came up with the idea of turning death into an industry. He was responsible for some of the worst things that happened during World War II. When things finally started looking bad for Germany, Eichmann fled to avoid arrest and trial. He hid out in a few places in Europe before things got too hot for him. Then he split for Argentina. I think they finally caught him and put him in prison. Or maybe they executed him. I'm not sure.

So there I was with an Argentinian passport for Klaus Adler, an old newspaper photo of some anonymous Nazi in full regalia and a hand-drawn map of a place that because of the passport Adam guessed was somewhere in Argentina.

I printed out the map and studied it. There were a couple of names scrawled on lines that looked like they might be streets.

I clicked into Google Maps and typed in one of the names and *Argentina*. I got a hit in Buenos Aires, in a district called San Telmo. It looked like Adam was right. I printed that map and then I went into Google Earth for a real-life look. Buenos Aires was pretty close. It should be easy to get there and check this out—even though it probably wouldn't pan out, not after all this time. The way I figured it, I'd do a hop, skip and a jump to San Telmo, then another hop, skip and a jump back home.

Piece of cake.

Turned out I was wrong.

THREE

Ed wasn't around when I shut down the computer. By then I had booked a flight from Montevideo to Buenos Aires—it was only forty minutes by air, according to the website I used, so I guess I could have waited until he came back. But the other guys were already on their missions. Who knew what I was going to find out or how long it would take?

I called for a cab, stuffed my things into my duffel bag and scrawled a note: *Had a great time. Thanks for the hospitality. Just heard from a friend in Buenos Aires. Going for a quick visit before heading home.*

It was early evening by the time I cleared customs at the airport in Buenos Aires. I flagged a cab and told the driver where I wanted to go. He dropped me at my destination, and the next thing I knew, I was walking down a narrow but bustling street and wondering what I was doing there. I mean, come on. That newspaper clipping? It was from 1945. The passport? It expired in 1963—before even the Major was born. And the little map in my hand, with the address on it? My guess was that it was about the same vintage as the passport. Suppose I had a map of, say, Toronto, from sometime in the early 1960s. How many streets would be the same, and how many would be different? What about the people? Would anyone who lived on a specific street back then still be living there now, fifty-plus years later? Who was I kidding? Everything would be different. People would have moved—or died. So what made me think I was going to find anything useful here, even assuming I managed to find the address from David McLean's old notebook?

Common sense told me there was no way I was going to strike gold. I was just going through the motions—doing it, I guess, for Adam, because he'd asked me. He and the other cousins had all been close to David McLean and were closer now after everything they'd gone through in the months since he'd died. Adam and the rest of them are part of a big family that's managed pretty well without me. I understand why they care so much about their grandfather's past. That's the way I still think of him—as *their* grandfather. My mother's mother had a relationship with David McLean after his wife died. She broke up with him before she knew she was pregnant. And, being one of those super-independent women—I bet she burned her bra back there during the early days of women's lib—she didn't see any point in mentioning that fact to him. After all, their relationship was over and she was perfectly capable of raising a child on her own. Which is what she did. McLean only found out about his fifth daughter (my mom)—and her son (me)—after my mom died. He read the obituary— a lot of old people read them—spotted my grandmother's name in it (he told me he'd been stunned), did the math and voilà!

David McLean turned out to be an okay guy. He'd wanted to meet me, and eventually he did.

I even stayed with him for a little while after I got in trouble with the Major and the law. He seemed nice. But his past? What did that matter to anyone, especially me, now that he was dead? That's what I told myself anyway. The truth? I was as curious as the rest of my cousins. What had the old man been up to? And where did Nazis figure in?

So there I was in Buenos Aires.

The street I was on was lined with rows of attached houses—or maybe they were apartments. The front doors opened right up onto the cobblestones. Occasionally a horn blared and I had to jump aside to let a car pass. There were people chatting here and there. A woman was attacking her front step with a scrub brush, a bucket of soapy water beside her. And then, there it was, the number I was looking for.

I approached the door. There was a bell pull. I rang it.

No answer.

I waited some more. Someone said something in Spanish. I turned and saw that the woman who'd been scrubbing her doorstep was standing now, scrub brush in hand, and that she was talking to me. She spoke again, louder this time. I had to concentrate hard on every word. She spoke Spanish with an accent I had never heard before, but I finally got it. She was telling me that there was no one home.

"Do you know the people who live here?" I asked, also in Spanish. She squinted at me, as if trying to see the words coming out of my mouth. I repeated the question more slowly.

"*Sí.*"

"Have they lived here a long time?"

"Five years. Maybe six."

Which meant that whoever the residents were now, they probably knew nothing about what had happened here fifty years ago.

I asked if she'd known the people who'd lived here before the most recent residents.

"*Sí.*" Apparently, they were a nice couple from the countryside. They were good neighbors for twenty years, until the man died in a car accident.

Twenty years meant that they hadn't been here in the 1960s either. Strike two.

"What about the people before that?" I asked.

The old woman didn't know. "*¿Es importante?*" she asked.

"*Sí. Muy importante.*"

27

She turned and shouted a name. A stout woman stopped in front of a house a little farther down the street. She had a key in one hand and two heavy bags of shopping in the other. The woman with the scrub brush said something to her, but she spoke so fast I didn't catch most of it. The woman with the groceries nodded. She set her bags down on the stoop so that she could unlock the door while she asked me what I wanted to know.

I told her I was looking for the people who had lived here a long time ago.

She smiled. "¿*Americano*?"

"Canadian." Maybe I'm not always as proud of it as I should be, but I'm proud enough when I'm traveling to make sure people get it right.

She switched to English, which she spoke better than I spoke Spanish. "My son-in-law, the second one, he is American," she said. "So, you are looking for Herr Franken?"

"Franken?"

"Heinrich Franken. This is who you are asking about, no?"

Heinrich Franken. The name definitely sounded German. Was it the name of the Nazi in the newspaper clipping? I thought about digging it out but hesitated. Adam had warned me not to tell anyone what I was up to. But he also wanted me to figure out what the phony passport was all about and what David McLean had been involved in. I couldn't do that if I couldn't figure out why this address was important and what, if anything, it had to do with Nazis.

"Have you lived on this street for a long time?" I asked the woman.

"Since I was born. It was my parents' house, and now it is mine."

"Do you know how long Herr Franken lived here?"

"He moved in with his wife and his son when I was a little girl. I was nine when he arrived and eleven when he moved to America."

"America?"

"We were envious. A man came to the house with an offer for Herr Franken to go and work in America. He had a German name, but I think he was American." She thought for a moment. "Yes. He was American. I remember Mirella—that was Herr Franken's wife—telling it to my mother. She said his name was Adler and that Adler is German for eagle, and the eagle is an important symbol in America."

Adler was the name on David McLean's passport. But why had he come here to offer an ex-Nazi a job in America? And why had he used an alias to do it?

"What kind of job was it?" I asked.

"It was at an airplane factory. In California. I was jealous of Mirella. California was where they had the movie stars, and I loved American movies. My father said that Herr Franken would be able to live like a king in America."

Yeah, those were the days. All those big factories worked overtime after the war, pouring out not just airplanes but also cars and refrigerators and televisions, all the things that people finally had the money to buy after a decade-long depression and then a world war.

I dipped into my pocket, pulled out the copy of the newspaper photo and unfolded it. But while I was doing that, something else fell to the ground. My copy of Klaus Adler's passport photo. The woman looked down at it.

"That is the American. That is Herr Adler." She sounded surprised. "I remember him. He was my first American, and he looked just like I imagined he would—so handsome."

I picked up the photo and showed her again.

"Are you sure, senora? Are you sure this is the American who offered a job to Mr. Franken?"

She was more than sure. She was positive.

I showed her the photo of the three German officers and pointed to the head that was circled.

"And this man? Do you recognize him?"

She stared at the photo, her face somber, and slowly nodded. "Herr Franken. My father was right. He said Herr Franken had probably been a Nazi. There were many of them here after the war. He was a quiet man, Herr Franken. Always kept to himself. His wife, she was different. She was Argentinian. She liked to talk."

I didn't absorb much after she made the positive identification.

"You are sure, senora?" I asked again. "This man here"—I thrust a finger at the circled head—"this is Herr Franken?"

"*Sí.*"

"And you think he went to the States, to California?"

"*Sí.* Mirella was so excited. She came to our house. She was always coming to our house, but only when

Herr Franken was not home. She was his second wife, you understand. She was very young and naive. My mother said that Herr Franken only married her because he needed someone to keep house for him and his son."

"Was the boy young?"

"Oh, no. He was grown up. Only a bit younger than Mirella. She was twenty-five when she married Herr Franken, and my mother thought it was a scandal that the old man married someone so much younger. She worked very hard, Mirella. But she never complained. When she found out they were going to America, she came to our house and she danced in our kitchen, she was so excited. She said it was a secret and that she wasn't supposed to tell, but she told us anyway. She went first, with Siegfried—"

"Siegfried?"

"Herr Franken's son. He and Mirella went ahead to get everything ready. Herr Franken followed a few days later with the American. My mother was sure that Mirella would send her a photograph of her new home, with a big picture window and a driveway with a car in it and a green yard all around the house."

"Did she?"

The woman shook her head. "But she wrote. One postcard, many years later."

"What did she say?"

"I don't remember. But she was sad."

"Sad?"

"Homesick. She wanted to come back home." She paused. "*Momento*." She disappeared into the house. I waited. The woman who was scrubbing her steps looked at me.

"Here." The woman was back with a large book in her hand. When she opened it, I saw that it was a stamp album. "My brother collected them." She crossed herself, so I guessed her brother was dead. "He would beg all the neighbors—all the Germans and the people who came from other countries and got letters from home." She leafed through the album until she found a small stack of postcards. She handed me the album so that she could search through them. "He liked the pictures. Here." She pulled one from the stack and handed it to me in exchange for the album. "This is from Mirella."

It was in Spanish, and the slanted handwriting was so tiny I could barely read it. The return address, though, was clear enough.

"This isn't from California," I said. The return address was in Detroit, Michigan.

"That is all we heard from her. She says she is lonely, but she doesn't say why," the woman said. "If you want, you can keep the card."

"Are you sure?"

"I remember when my mother got it. She read it and gave it to my brother, and the only thing she ever said is that she supposed Mirella got what any foolish girl deserved. I didn't understand at the time what she meant, and my mother didn't explain. But now I think it must have something to do with that picture you showed me. Now I think Mirella learned what kind of man her husband was. Take it. I have no use for it."

I thanked the woman, pocketed the postcard and my pictures, and headed back the way I had come. It wasn't long before I was at the airport, lucking into a flight to Detroit with a stopover in Miami, sixteen hours in all. While I waited to go through security, I wondered again why on earth my grandfather had come to Argentina to offer a job to an ex-Nazi. Who had he been working for? The airplane manufacturer? Suppose that was it. Suppose Franken had been some kind of engineer in Germany before the war, and suppose the airplane manufacturer had wanted to recruit him? It was possible. But why had my grandfather used an alias? And why a German alias? It didn't make sense.

I boarded my flight, taking my duffel bag as carry-on. The Major has a massive aversion to checking baggage. It's a waste of time, as far as he's concerned, to stand around some arrivals carousel, waiting for your suitcase to appear or, in a whole lot of cases (no pun intended), not appear at all. So he packs light. And since I'd traveled with him as far as Uruguay, and me wasting my time equaled him wasting his time, I'd also packed light. Which was no problem, because it's hot in Uruguay when it's butt-freezing weather up in the Great White North.

To get the flight I wanted, I had to book business class. I put it on the Major's credit card, which he'd given me because I was going to have to make my own way home anyway after he shipped out, and you never knew what could happen. If you're the Major, you don't want your son stranded somewhere in South America without a peso to his name. My ticket gave me access to a special lounge, which, let me tell you, was not just a step but a whole flight of stairs above the service—or complete lack of service offered to passengers who fly economy. (In case you're wondering, I wasn't worried about how the Major would react to his next credit card statement. As promised, Adam had transferred some money into my bank account, and it was more than enough to cover my expenses.) While I was in the lounge, I worked on my customs form. I struggled a little over what to write in the space that asks where you'll be staying in the United States. The Americans want to know exactly where to find you in that big old land of the free, in case you turn out to be a terrorist or something. I wrote in the name of a hotel near the Detroit airport—thank God for business-class Internet services, complete with computer access. I prayed no one would check until and unless they had a compelling reason to.

I ate better than I ever imagined possible on an airplane. I watched part of a movie, but it didn't hold my interest. I slept. I slept. I slept.

It was morning when the plane landed in Miami.

I got off and followed the herd to US Customs and Border Protection. I figured I was a natural to get waved through. After all, I'm Canadian. Canadians have a totally nonthreatening image.

It didn't work out the way I expected.

I got pulled aside. I was told to point out my stuff—my duffel and a tray containing my belt, my shoes, a bunch of change (Uruguayan, Argentinian and Canadian) and my cell phone—"but don't touch anything," the guard warned. What did she—a very surly she—think I was? A drug smuggler?

I realized with a jolt that maybe she thought exactly that. I was young, male, kinda scruffy, if you want to know the truth, and traveling alone from South America. Profile or what?

I got hauled into a small room. My stuff did not immediately follow me. They made me sit for nearly an hour, and I started to worry I'd miss my connecting flight. I knew what that was all about. Make them wait equals make them stew equals make them think they're in a manure pile so deep they'll have to shovel for a year to get out. In other words, make them sweat.

It worked. I sweated. I didn't need or want any trouble, especially not with US Border Protection. Those guys are deeply suspicious, hard-core tenacious and 100 percent humorless.

Finally, a man appeared. Not a uniform, but a suit. He stepped into the room, waited until the door clicked shut behind him and then stood there, my passport and a file folder in his hand, eyeballing me like he was a cop and I was the killer he'd been searching for all his life, like that cop in *Les Misérables*, one of the zillions of musicals my grandma has dragged me to. He flipped open my passport to the photo page and stared at it as if he was checking it for the first time. But I'm no rookie. I live with the Major, Mister Military Police, Criminal Investigations Unit. I know a dodge when I see it.

"Rennie Charbonneau," he said, hanging a big question mark in the air like for sure the name on my passport was an alias.

"That's right. And you are?" Because I was not going to let this guy intimidate me. No way.

"Bill Jones." Said with a pinched smile.

Bill Jones? And he's acting like Rennie Charbonneau is a phony name?

Mr. Jones sat down across the table from me. "I see you were in Argentina."

Wow, the guy could read a customs stamp.

I waited.

"What were you doing in Argentina, Rennie?"

"Seeing the sights, *Bill*."

He bridled when I used his first name, but he didn't say anything about it.

"And before that you were in Uruguay."

Since he said this flat—a statement, not a question—to show me, I guess, just how sharp his reading skills were, I didn't see a need to comment.

Silence.

"What were you doing in Uruguay, Rennie?"

"Seeing more sights, Bill."

This time he locked eyes with me. "Bit of a smart-ass, huh?"

My answer: a smart-ass shrug. Why disappoint?

He reached into the folder and brought out my customs form. "Says here you're taking a connecting flight to Detroit. What's in Detroit for you, Rennie?"

"Just want to see—"

"—the sights. That answer is getting old, son." He leaned back in his chair and did the thing cops like to do—he looked at me like he was studying me and then gave a little nod, like Okay, Sonny Boy, I've got your number.

The door opened. A head poked in. Bill stepped out of the room. He was back a moment later with my duffel and the tray with my shoes and other stuff. He set them on the table and sat down again.

"One more time, Rennie. What's in Detroit for you?"

I didn't want to play games anymore. I just wanted to get out of there. "I was on vacation with my dad, and now I'm on my way home."

"Via Detroit."

"My grandmother is meeting me there. We're going to stay over and then drive up to see some friends of hers in Windsor. That's in Canada." It was also a lie—the meeting my grandmother part, I mean.

"I see. You ever been in any trouble with the police, Rennie?"

I guessed he knew the answer to that. I guessed that's why he'd yanked me out of the line. I guessed that was what the waiting was all about.

"Yeah."

"Tell me about it."

I gave him the short course.

"Ever done drugs?"

"No."

"Trafficked them?"

"I don't have a record for that, if that's what you mean."

"It's not."

"No, I've never sold drugs." Geez.

His eyes drilled into mine for a full minute, maybe longer.

"Okay. You're free to go." Just like that—now that I'd been run through whatever databases they check and had barely enough time to make my flight. Still, I was glad to get out of there.

FOUR

So that's how—and why—I ended up in Detroit with a shotgun pointed at my back.

Well, that's most of it.

When I landed, I went online again and did a search on the address Mirella had included on her one and only communication with her neighbors back home. That's how I found out who lived there now. I wasn't surprised to find that the phone number listed for the address didn't belong to anyone named Franken. It belonged to a C. Forrester. But was Mr. (or Mrs. or Ms.) Forrester a new resident or an old one? If he (or she or they) had been there long enough, they might know the people who'd lived there before. Maybe C. Forrester knew where the old resident had gone. Hey, it had worked in Argentina. Maybe my luck would hold in Detroit.

That's what I thought at the time—before I heroically (in my humble opinion) broke into the house and got mistaken for an invader.

"I'm not an intruder, I swear," I say to the armed guy behind me without turning around. I'm not about to make any moves, never mind sudden ones, when there's a loaded weapon pointed at my back. "I saw the old man—"

Something jabs me hard in the spine. It's the barrel of that shotgun, I know it. I feel cold all over and then go numb. I pray I don't wet myself.

"Put the gun down, Gerry," the old man says. "The boy was helping me."

"Helping you what?" the voice behind me growls.

"He fell," I say, wasting no time getting in on the put-the-gun-down bandwagon. "I thought he might have had a heart attack or something."

The gun pulls away from my spine, and the man holding it circles around me to get a good look. He's shorter than me, but wide at the shoulders and chest and with very little gut, like maybe he works out. His hair is buzzed short and salted with gray. His jaw is stubbled. His mouth is pulled down into a frown that the lines etched into his face suggest is more or less permanent. Both of his hands are wrapped around the shotgun, ready to hoist it and take aim again if he feels he has to. His eyes glance away from me for no more than a split second while he says, "What happened, Dad? Do you have chest pain?"

The old man bats the thought away like a pesky fly. "I stumbled and fell, that's all."

"It looked like you were unconscious," I say. I raise my hand to pull off the ridiculous hat I'm wearing. I bought it at the airport after I realized my tuque was missing. It's cold in Detroit in late December, the damp kind of cold that seeps right into your bones. But when I start to reach up, Gerry tenses and the next thing I know, that shotgun is pointed at me again. I decide to leave the hat on my still-intact head.

The shotgun dips slightly in Gerry's hands. His eyes go back to the old man. "*Were* you unconscious, Dad?"

The old man dodges the question. "I'm fine. There's nothing to worry about." His watery eyes zero in on me. "Why did you come here?"

"I told you. I saw—"

His hand slices through the air to cut me off. "You couldn't possibly have seen me from the street, not if I was on the floor." Clutching his wheeled walker, he glides in so close that I can smell his sour breath. "I don't want to have to ask you again: why did you come here?"

I hear footsteps again and another voice, a female one this time. She sounds panicky. "Uncle Gerry? Grandpa? Are you here? What happened to the door? Is Eric all right?"

"In here," Gerry calls.

"I asked you a question." The old man presses closer so that all I can see is his lined face. It's like a gigantic relief map. A map to nowhere pleasant.

I figure there are two ways to go here. I can improvise, or I can tell the truth. Two angry men and one loaded shotgun make me want to go with the first option—*sorry, I must have got the wrong address; I'm new in town and I got lost*—and get the hell out of there. But I'm here for a reason.

"I'm looking for someone," I say. "A woman. I think she used to live here."

"Nobody has lived here except Dad," Gerry says. "If that's the best you can come up with—"

"She was from South America. Her name was—"

"I already told you, no one has ever lived here except for my father." Gerry sounds ready to heft the shotgun again.

"Uncle Gerry?"

It's a girl a couple of years older than me at the most. She doesn't look like she belongs here. She's dressed too nicely, like someone out of a magazine, not at all like Uncle Gerry, who is in a plaid shirt, jeans, and work boots, or the old man, who is wearing pajamas, a raggedy robe and beat-up slippers.

"It's okay, Katya," Gerry says. "I've got this under control." He turns to me. "So, according to you, you got the wrong house." He raises the shotgun. "Well, you can say that again, sport. The only question is, do I turn you over to the cops for breaking and entering, or do I deal with you myself?"

"Who *is* that?" Katya is not nearly as alarmed by the shotgun as I think she should be. "What's going on, Uncle Gerry?"

"Intruder," Gerry says.

"No! It's not like that." I have my hands over my head in a pose I like to call please-please-*please* don't-kill-me. "I'm looking for someone. I only broke in—"

"See? He admits it!"

If you ask me, Gerry is looking for an excuse to blast me.

"Who's he looking for?" Katya asks as if I'm not standing right in front of her. "Does this have something to do with Eric?"

"He *says* he's looking for some woman who used to live here," Gerry says, like he's daring me to pull his other leg.

"What woman?" Katya looks to her grandfather for an explanation.

"Her name was Mirella," I say quickly. Keep talking and maybe Uncle Gerry won't shoot. "She sent a postcard with this address on it."

I swear Gerry is going to rack the slide of that shotgun again. I pray his only intention is to march me out of his castle. But I'll never know because the old man, Gerry's dad, says, "Did you say Mirella?"

"You know her?" Gerry and I say at exactly the same time.

The old man looks at us, surprised, but I'm not sure why. He has the same chagrined expression on his face as Grand-père when he blurts out something and then realizes he shouldn't have. It's what

Grand-mère calls letting his tongue get ahead of his brain.

"If it's the same Mirella," he mumbles. "But that was a long time ago."

"The postcard she sent from here was mailed in the sixties," I say.

The old man nods. "I haven't thought about her in a long time."

"So you do know her," Gerry says.

"She was here, but not for long."

Gerry looks puzzled. "I don't remember that."

"It was before you were born. She came here from California, but she was originally from South America, as I recall." He's got a dreamy, remembering look in his eyes.

"She was from Argentina." I'm excited. I'm on the right track. I have a lead. At least, I think I do.

"Who was she?" Gerry asks.

The old man stares at him. He wobbles a little, and Katya takes one of his arms.

"She...she was a friend of a friend of your mother's," he says. "She heard about the jobs here in the auto industry and came east to find work. But she didn't know anyone and needed a place to stay until she could find something." He smiles a little. "Mirella. She was a good person. Kind."

"Do you know what happened to her?" I ask. "Do you know where she is now?"

He shakes his head. "I gave her a few leads. So did Lucille, my wife. She eventually found something—I don't remember where. Maybe my wife saw her again, but I never did. Like I said, it was a long time ago."

"Why are you looking for her?" Katya asks. The suspicion in her voice matches her narrowed eyes. Given the smashed doorframe, the broken lock and the shotgun, I don't blame her. If I were her, I'd be wondering who I was and what I was doing in her house.

All three of them are staring at me, waiting for my answer to Katya's question. I don't know what to say. Gerry glances at the old man. The old man keeps his eyes on me.

"I should turn you in," Gerry growls.

The old man takes a different tack.

"The boy helped me," he says. Water is seeping from his eyes—not tears, just old-man eye water—but apart from that, they're as sharp as lasers. "Make me a coffee, Gerry. Strong, not the watery slop you like.

And you." He means me. "You can help me to my room."

Gerry hangs uncertainly in the passageway, the shotgun hovering between his shoulder and his waist. The old man wraps one hand around the barrel and lowers it. He wheels himself past.

"Grandpa—?" Katya begins.

"Not now, Katya."

The old man steers his roller-walker past the stairs and down a narrow hall to a door. He pushes it open, slides inside and stands there waiting for me to enter. But I stay where I am, too stunned by what I see to move.

The old man catches me by the arm and pulls me in. His fingers are bony and strong. It feels like a living skeleton has clamped hold of me. Once I'm inside, all I can do is stare. The place is like a museum—a small one, but crammed from floor to ceiling with stuff. Some of the stuff is mounted on the walls—weapons mostly, daggers, bayonets, old rifles, handguns—and when I look closely at it, I see swastikas. Some of the stuff is in framed cases, also mounted on the walls. Inside are medals, badges, epaulets and brass buttons. They also have swastikas on them. There are posters and photographs—really old, all German, all from the Nazi era. There are a couple of mannequins in full uniform—one in black, one in brown. One's a pretty sharp-looking officer, if you overlook the swastikas. On shelves there are more military hats and helmets. There are German beer mugs that look like what you'd see in the old days of World War II. There's a pair of field binoculars with a beat-up leather case. There's a pilot's jacket and helmet, totally old-school. There are grenades, which I hope aren't live. There are displays of insignia and dog tags. There are belt buckles, with and without the belts, leather holsters, with and without guns. There are coins, lapel pins and a swastika'd watch. There are flags and pennants, some of them hanging down from the ceiling, some of them on the walls, and some of them neatly folded and sealed in plastic bags. There are super-old magazines and newspapers, all in German. A lot of them have Adolf Hitler on the cover. There are bunches of official-looking documents, little booklets that look like passports but turn out to be work permits, travel permits, identification papers and ration documents. And books. Dozens of them. Maybe hundreds. Stacked on the floor and overflowing bookshelves.

I turn slowly as I take it all in. When I look back at the old man, he's smiling.

"Pretty impressive, huh?"

"Were you in the war?"

He laughs. "I may look old to you, but I was too young to serve. You've heard of D-Day, young man?"

I nod. "Sure. My dad's in the military." The Major is not only a career soldier, but he's pretty sharp on military history. You don't want to get him started on specific battles and tactics, trust me. Once he gets wound up, he won't stop until he's reenacted whatever battle it was and critiqued the strategy and tactics on both sides. It's about the only topic on which he will deliver more than a sentence at a time—if you don't count when he's reaming me out for something.

"My father was there at D-Day. He was there during the march on Berlin too," He glances around. "He collected some of this. A lot of soldiers did. Souvenirs of their times overseas. But I doubt many of them collected on this scale. I picked up the rest over the years."

"It's a lot of stuff," I concede.

"When Gerry moved in with the kids, he wanted me to get rid of it all. Alice, my daughter, died twelve years ago, so Gerry and I took on the kids." I wonder what happened to Alice's husband, but he doesn't say and I don't ask. "Clutter, that's what Gerry calls this. Trash. But I told him, this is my house, not yours. And these things belonged to my father—they meant something to him." He shuffles over to the bed and drops down onto it. "You're a young fellow. Imagine if you went to war. And not just any war, but one that really mattered. One that involved just about the whole world. And imagine you survived it—survived all those years. Because when men went to war then, young man—"

"Rennie," I say. "My name is Rennie."

"Pleased to meet you, Rennie. I'm Curtis. Curtis Forrester." He thrusts out a hand and we shake. "When men—or should I say boys—went to war in those days, they went for the duration. And a lot of them didn't come back. But my father did. He came back."

Katya appears with two mugs of coffee. She hands one to Curtis and shoves one in my general direction.

"I didn't know what you take," she says. She pulls something from her pocket—one of those plastic pill containers that are divided into days of the week.

She opens the one for today and shakes half a dozen pills into the old man's hand. "It's time for you to rest, Grandpa."

The old man takes the pills without argument. "I have to do what this lovely young lady tells me," he says. He beams at her, and it's obvious he adores his granddaughter. "Come back, Rennie," he tells me. He sticks out his hand again, and I go closer to shake it. "Come back and visit. No one around here is interested in any of my stories."

"That's not true, Grandpa," Katya says. There's a lilt in her voice, the kind a parent uses with a small child. A jollying note. She's indulging him, like a mother drinking imaginary tea from a doll-sized teacup at her little girl's make-believe tea party.

"They think they've heard it all," the old man says. "Even this granddaughter of mine, who moved away and hardly ever comes for a visit. Come back, Rennie. Keep an old man company."

I nod, to be polite. I swallow some coffee, also to be polite. It's too sweet and too milky. Then I let Katya hustle me out of the room and down the corridor to the front door where Gerry, cursing to himself, is trying to repair the damage I did. He glowers at me when I pass, and I edge clear of him and the hammer he's wielding.

Katya follows me outside and down to the sidewalk, even though she's not dressed for the cold.

"Thank you for helping my grandfather," she says.

"No problem."

"But it would be best if you don't come back. He's old and sick. He needs his rest."

"You should probably get him checked out by a doctor. He was unconscious when I found him."

"I will. You don't have to worry about that."

"He sure seems interested in World War Two."

"He thinks he knows everything there is to know. Now, if you'll excuse me."

And even if I don't, apparently, because she turns and runs up the walkway and into the house.

FIVE

I trudge up the street. It's late, and I have nowhere to stay. I'm not even entirely sure where I am. I got a taxi to drop me here from the airport, but I don't see any cabs around now. I don't see any cars at all.

I'm thinking about the old man. He knew Mirella—assuming it's the same Mirella. Mirella from South America, he said, via California. She stayed there for a while maybe fifty years ago, judging by my rough estimate of Gerry's age. I'd been thinking of her all this time as a young girl from Buenos Aires, but I realize now that if she's still alive, she's in her mid-seventies. She's my grandma's age. But it wasn't the same for her here as it was back home. Back home, she had roots. She had friends and neighbors, people who knew her and who she confided in. But here? She came here from California alone, according to Curtis. Where was her husband when she made the trip to Detroit? Where was Heinrich Franken?

I have to go back, I realize. I have to talk to the old man again. Maybe he doesn't know anything, but maybe he can point me in a direction. Back in the sixties, Detroit was booming. The car plants were working overtime. Auto-parts plants too. The jobs were well paying. Maybe Mirella ended up in one of them. If she did, maybe someone has a record of her.

If she's still alive.

I tromp up the street, tired, hungry and, all of a sudden, very cold.

What a place! I've never been in a city that looks so much like the countryside. This is supposed to be Motor City, but it looks more like Farmville. This is the place where Ford and General Motors and Chrysler built cars for decades—in Ford's case, for almost a century. But where I am, you'd never know it.

I keep walking.

My mind flashes back to the ocean and the sun and all the pretty senoritas in their little bikinis on the beach back in Uruguay. I think about one in particular, a raven-haired beauty the same age as me—seventeen—with big brown eyes that sparkled with delight when I hit a clown's nose straight on, ten times in a row, at a carnival booth down by the ocean. I think about the kiss she gave me when I presented her kid brother with an armful of prizes, all his choice, while people clapped and the carny at the booth scowled, convinced I had cheated somehow. But really, how can you cheat at throwing a softball? You either have the arm—and the eye—or you don't. I have them both.

I walk.

I think about my grandma—my mom's mom—in her comfy downtown condo in midtown Toronto. I was supposed to meet her there after the Major shipped out. The plan: New Year's Eve dinner at one of the swankiest restaurants in town, followed by a celebration complete with dancing. Grandma loves to make me dance with her. She says she loves the look of panic and embarrassment on my face as I try to keep up with her. Geez!

I walk.

I think about the stuff Adam emailed me—the passport photo, the newspaper clipping, the indecipherable notes, the hand-drawn map—and how crazy it all is, and I wonder why I didn't tell him, "Sorry, compadre, no can do." I mean, six months ago, I had no idea who Adam was. But here's the thing. After those crazy missions David McLean sent us on, Adam was the one cousin who decided to keep in touch, and pretty soon, despite my best intentions, I got to like him. He's okay. All of my cousins on my mom's side of the family turned out to be okay. Who knew?

I walk.

I think about my grandfather. Not Grand-père, the Major's dad, but David McLean, the guy who sent me to Iceland after he died. I think about freezing my butt off there too. I almost died when I was dumped on a glacier and a snowstorm struck. I look around me now. Is this just a coincidence, or is it some kind of cosmic plot? Because here I am in the ice and snow again.

I walk.

Then I stop.

There's a knot of guys up ahead, huddled around a fire in what looks like an old garbage can or oil drum. Beyond them, I see streetlights. I even see some neon, a sure sign that I'm about to exit urban country neighborhood and enter urban commercial district.

One of the guys is facing in my direction. He nudges the guy next to him. One by one, all six of them turn to look at me. They're all African-American—at least, I assume they are. This comes as no surprise. Another thing I know about Detroit—it's 85 percent black. I'm not prejudiced or anything. They could be six white guys huddled around a fire in an oil drum, and I'd still be cautious. It's common sense, right? Guys who cozy up to oil drums for warmth on frigid December nights tend to be either fiscally challenged (otherwise they'd be somewhere indoors) or up to no good. Plus there's a bunch of them and just one of me. And did I mention how dark it is with no working streetlamps?

I think about wheeling around and cutting across to the next block to avoid trouble. But two of the guys have already taken a step away from the fire and toward me. And anyway, if I detour off this street,

I won't be any better off. I'll still be in the dark, and if they decide to follow me, it'll still be six against one.

I pull myself up tall, walk straight toward them. And I say, "*Saluts, mes amis. Comment ça va?*"

The two guys in front glance at each other. One gets all squinty-eyed.

"Tourist." A grin edges across his face. "Yo, where you from?"

I suddenly wish I was back on the beach with that dark-eyed senorita in her teeny-tiny bikini.

"I asked you a question," he says. The way the others all look at him, I figure he's the main guy.

A second guy, his expression more curious than predatory, jerks his chin. "*D'où viens-tu?*"

He has an accent that's nothing like mine. It's also nothing like my grandparents' or like anyone else's I ever heard when the Major was based in Quebec. It's definitely nothing like the acccent of any French teacher I ever had outside of Quebec, most of whom were from France and insisted on *Académie de la langue française*-type French. No, this guy is from somewhere else.

"*Côte d'Ivoire, n'est-ce pas?*" I say.

The guy smiles. Then he laughs. "*Oui, oui.*" He nods enthusiastically. "*Côte d'Ivoire. Tu l'a visité?*"

"*Malheureusement non.*" I've never visited Ivory Coast. But, thank God, I've been with the Major on countless occasions when he's heard some cab driver or gas jockey or convenience-store clerk utter a few words and has homed right in on his accent like one of those heat-seeking missiles. People are always tickled when he recognizes a Kurdish or Haitian or Belarus accent when, they figure, most people have no idea where to locate those places on a map. It gives the Major instant rapport.

"*Et que fais-tu ici*?" Ivory Coast guy asks. What are you doing here?

"You're in America," Squinty-Eyes says. "Speak American, Jack."

"It's Jacques, not Jack." Ivory Coast rolls his eyes and looks at me as if he expects me to understand how annoying it is when people mangle his name. I do.

"I'm looking for someplace to stay." I direct this not to all six guys, but only to Jacques. "You know somewhere cheap? A youth hostel maybe?" I hope by asking this last question, they'll get the idea that I'm broke, even though I'm not.

Squinty-Eyes immediately loses interest, which is okay by me.

"What do we look like?" he says. "The Tourist Information Center?" He nudges the guy next to him, and they brush by me, every one of them except Jacques jostling me as they pass.

Whatever. I shrug deeper into my jacket and keep walking. I'm thinking about the house Mirella sent her postcard from and why I'm here and what Nazis have to do with it and what I'm supposed to do and whether I even want to do it. I cross street after street, scanning for someplace, any place, I can get a room or a bed or just a patch of warmth. Then—don't you know it—someone grabs me from behind.

My heart slams in my chest. But, thanks to the Major, my muscles remember all on their own what they're supposed to do. I tell myself that if he's armed (in this town, the probability is up around 90-plus percent), I'm screwed. But if he isn't, well then he's in for some major hurt before he gets what he wants from me—*if* he gets it.

I spin around. It's Jacques. He laughs. It's a deep belly laugh.

"I did not mean to frighten you," he says, this time in Côte-d'Ivoire accented English. "I wanted to tell you—you can stay at my place."

"Yeah?"

He nods and switches back to French. "I don't get much chance to speak French. These Americans, they're all the same. *Speak American*, as if that's even a language. Come on. It's not far."

We walk a couple more blocks and then stop in front of a broken-down house that stands like the lone tooth in an otherwise toothless mouth. What is it with this town?

"This is your place?" I ask. No offense to him— gift horse, mouth, etc.—but what a dump.

"I live here. But is it my place?" He shrugs. "The jobs disappeared. The bosses, they send the work to places where they can pay a few dollars a day. The people who lived here, they don't live here anymore. It's not much. But it has a roof and walls."

He leads me up a groaning porch, shoulders the front door to unstick it and strides through the front hall toward the back of the house. If it wasn't for that clear sky, those stars and that slice of moon, I'd be tripping and stumbling and maybe falling flat on my face. He stops in front of another door and digs something out of his pocket. A key. He inserts it into a padlock, opens the door, and suddenly there's light. I blink as I take in the surroundings.

The paint, where I can see it, is peeling off the walls. The floor—again, where I can see it—is covered with cracked linoleum. But mostly I can't see it any more than I can see the walls, which are covered with bright wall hangings and rugs, crazy-patterned in primary colors. A half dozen equally colorful throw rugs cover most of the floor. A bare lightbulb hangs at the end of a cord dangling from the ceiling. The one thing I have no problem seeing is my breath. It's cold in here.

Jacques turns on a space heater. "We keep just enough heat in the house so the pipes don't freeze." He waves me onto a heap of mattresses covered with a thick quilt. "The rest—it's up to each of us."

"Us?"

"There are other people living here, each with a room."

As if on cue, I hear a bass line from up above.

"That is Hector," Jacques says. "A musician, when he can get work." He looks at the ceiling as the bass stops, then starts again, repeating the same few phrases, then stops again. If it bothers Jacques, he doesn't show it. "Sit. I'll make food."

He opens the window, letting in a blast of cold air, and pulls in a bucket with a lid on it. He dumps the contents into a pot, drops the pot onto a hotplate, and before long the cozy room is filled with a spicy, mouthwatering aroma. My stomach growls. The last food I ate was on the airplane, and that was nearly twenty-four hours ago. I lean back against the mound of pillows on the mattress and listen as Jacques tells me about his home in Côte d'Ivoire and the dreams that brought him to America. I'm on the verge of dozing off when he thrusts a plate and a spoon into my hand. He sits cross-legged on the mattress beside me and we both start to devour a spicy stew made with chickpeas and onions and—

"What kind of meat is this?" I ask.

"Goat. It's goat."

Pretty damn good goat, if you ask me.

I don't know when I fall asleep. But when I wake up, I'm under the quilt, sun is streaming through the window, Jacques is gone, and there's a note propped up on the windowsill. I find the bathroom—it's on the second floor, and it's pretty raw. Looks like none of the "tenants" share the Army mentality that's been ingrained in me by the Major. Back home, our bathroom glistens. Honest. I wash up.

Jacques's note tells me to lock up and deliver the key to him at work. I shoulder my duffel and head out. I'm surprised to find out that Jacques has a job and yet lives in a place like this. I thought maybe he was on welfare.

The directions lead me to a restaurant. Actually, it's more like a greasy spoon—a little place with battered booths along one wall, a few tables up front and a few more in the back, and stools at the counter. Jacques, it turns out, is the cook. He flashes a toothy grin at me and sends through a couple of fried eggs, a couple of slices of what's called Canadian bacon down here, a mountain of fried potatoes, and some toast. The waitress, a youngish woman with deep circles under her eyes but an easy smile, pours me some coffee and slides a bowl of individual creamers in front of me.

"You cook African food here?" I ask Jacques in French.

"I speak American here. To be polite to the customers. And to Elsie, who speaks American." He nods at the waitress.

"And Spanish. And Russian. And a few other languages." Elsie picks up some orders.

"But not the most civilized language in the world," Jacques says.

"For your information, my Latin is excellent," Elsie retorts.

Jacques laughs. "Elsie, this is Rennie."

"Hey, Rennie." She bustles by me to a booth where three black guys are sitting. They're older men, and they're dressed for the cold, like they work construction or maybe they used to. It's hard to tell in this town. Could be they work demolition.

"What's she doing waitressing here if she speaks so many languages?" I ask.

"For your information, I have a PhD," Elsie replies, scooting past me to grab a coffeepot and some mugs. "In linguistics. But you gotta make a living somehow, right, Jacques?"

I glance at Jacques.

"Right," Elsie says. "He didn't tell you. Jacques has an engineering degree. But he can't get a job here. No American experience."

Jacques just shrugs.

I look around the place. It's plain but clean, and the food smells great.

"Do a lot of people live around here?" I ask. "Because there seem to be a lot of houses missing."

"It's because of the car factories," Jacques says. "They laid off people; then they shut down."

"It wasn't just the car plants," Elsie chimes in. "All the auto-parts places closed too."

"People walked away from their houses," Jacques says. "They couldn't pay the mortgage anymore. They couldn't sell their places either. Everyone who could find something somewhere else moved. The people who stayed—if they had work, it didn't pay nearly as much as their old jobs, so they either abandoned their homes or let them fall into disrepair."

"It's pretty depressing," I say. "No offense."

"It's getting a little better," someone says. It's one of the construction workers. "People are trying."

"*Some* people are trying," one of his buddies says.

"Those urban farms, they're a good idea," the first guy says.

"Urban farms?" What's he talking about?

"Where there are a lot of empty lots. Some people are planting crops. We have great produce around here in the summer. Fresh. Local."

"We also have all those stray dogs," says the second guy. "Fifty thousand of them."

I can't help it—I whistle. "That's a lot of strays."

"You can say that again. Especially when the animal shelters have room for only fifteen thousand at the most."

"We also got those white-power jokers," says the third maybe-construction worker, who up until now has been silent.

"Idiots, the whole lot of them," another guy says.

"*Dangerous* idiots. They killed those two college kids."

"Some white-power guys *killed* someone?" This is some city. "Seriously? You mean, like, KKK guys?"

"Something like that," the third guy, the quiet one, says. He looks me up and down, and suddenly I feel very white. "They call themselves the Black Legion.

Attacked a couple of college kids. Beat one of them to death. Shot the other one."

"Man, those guys are crazy, *complètement fou*," Jacques says.

"They're cowards." Elsie, over beside the construction workers' booth now, slams down a re-up of toast as if to emphasize the point. "You know where they hold their rallies? In the suburbs, where most people are white."

"I'd like to see them hold one of those rallies in my neighborhood." He holds up his mug for more coffee. "I'd put my boot right up a skinny white ass or two."

I glance at the boots in question. They're steel-toed.

"What happened to the guys who killed those kids? Are they in prison?"

One of the construction workers snorts. "They ain't even been arrested."

"Why not? Don't the cops know who they are?"

"They know. They know exactly who they are. But they say they have no proof. Haven't even made an arrest, and it's been almost a year now."

"I see one of those kids around here all the time," another guy says. "Struttin'. He's always struttin', like he's cock of the walk. He's got away with murder, and he knows it. Thinks it makes him someone special. A real tough guy."

"An ignorant so-called tough guy. Kid's a school dropout. So are his buddies. Unemployed too. Living off the state. We're paying that kid's way. That's the thing that galls me."

The more I hear about this town, the more I want to get my business done and go home.

I eat up. When I try to pay, Jacques waves away my money. I hand him his key.

"Keep it," he said. "You are welcome in my home."

"You've done too much already." But I have one more favor to ask. "Can I leave my bag here—until I find a place?"

"No problem."

I hand it over.

Then I head back to the house where the old man lives.

SIX

A few words about Detroit, in case you don't know the place. Back when Mirella wrote her letter, the Big Three car makers ruled the world, and the guys who did the grunt work on the assembly line made out like kings (relatively—it's always relative), thanks to their union, which they'd had to fight long and hard to get. This is according to one of the brochures I picked up at the Welcome to Detroit kiosk at the airport.

How best to describe the city now? Here's some of what I found out: Back in the heyday of car manufacturing, Detroit was home to two million men, women and children. Today there are maybe 700,000 souls still living there, along with 90,000 abandoned buildings—houses, factories, stores, office buildings, you name it—that account for 5,000 acres of vacant land. Try and find that in some other big city. This place tells you all you need to know about history, namely that everything changes; nothing stays the same.

When I go back to the Forrester house and look at it in the clear light of day, I see how ramshackle it is. The doorframe has been fixed with some old wood, but so far it hasn't been painted. There's an old pickup truck in the driveway. Probably Gerry's. If it is, then he's probably home, and I'm not eager to run into him again. But the old man extended an invitation, and there's a chance he knows something.

I steel myself. I think about all the crazy things my cousins did because our grandfather asked them to. DJ climbed Mount Kilimanjaro. Spencer ended up being chased by gangsters. What would they say if they found out I was afraid to climb a few rickety steps?

I climb them.

I ring the doorbell. I don't hear anything, so I also knock.

A young guy with a shaved head, dressed in a hoodie and jeans, with Doc Marten boots or some knockoff version, answers the door. There are two other guys behind him. Together they make a V, my clue that the first guy is the boss and the other two are his wingmen. His muscle.

"What?" the main guy says.

I remember Katya from the night before. I remember what she asked her uncle.

"You're Eric," I say.

That catches him off guard.

"Do I know you?"

"We haven't met, if that's what you mean. But I was here last night. I met your uncle and your sister. And your granddad."

He nods right away. "You're that guy. You kicked down the door."

"I thought your granddad had a heart attack or something."

"Right." Like he doesn't believe me. What does he think—that I kicked down the door to rob the place? Of what? Probably the most valuable stuff in there is the old man's collection, but what kind of burglar would go for Nazi memorabilia? You go for cash, jewelry or electronics. Stuff that you can pawn or fence.

Come to think of it, what kind of burglar kicks in a front door?

The three of them look like bouncers at some high-end club, standing guard against the nonglamorous.

"Is your granddad here?" I ask. A stupid question. Where else would the old man be? "He asked me to come by."

Eric tilts his shaved head to one side. "He did, huh?" Again like he doesn't believe me.

"Tell him Rennie's here."

"Rennie?"

"Yeah."

Eric doesn't move. Instead, he nods at one of his pals, a guy with a skull tattoo on one side of his neck. Skull shuffles into the interior of the house. Eric looks me up and down, like he's a cop trying to rattle a perp. He doesn't do a very good job of it. My experience: when a cop stares down a perp, he's mostly got a look of disgust on his face, like he can't believe the kind of garbage he has to deal with. Eric, though, he's all suspicion, probably wondering why I'm here, why I want to speak to the old man, why I really kicked down the door.

Skull is back with mild surprise on his face. "He says to send him in."

The surprise migrates to Eric's face. He rakes me over with new interest before stepping aside with a sweep of his hand, like some smart-ass castle gate-keeper reluctantly making way for the servant of a duke or an earl.

I bend to unlace my boots.

"You can leave them on," Eric says.

Okay then. I head down the corridor to the old man's room. I'm sure I feel Eric's eyes on my back, but when I glance over my shoulder, the door is closed and Eric and his buddies are gone. I put him out of my mind. He has nothing to do with why I'm here. I knock on the old man's door.

"Come in."

Curtis is dressed in sweatpants and slippers, with a ratty old cardigan sweater over a long-sleeved T-shirt. His thin white hair is sticking out wildly, and his chin is stubbled. But he smiles a welcome as he hunts for something.

"Aha!" He holds it up. It's a bell with a wooden handle, like the ones you see in one-room school-houses in old movies. He picks it up by the handle and shakes it. A few seconds later the door opens, and Katya appears. Her eyes go straight to her grandfather.

"Is everything okay, Grandpa?" Then she sees me. "Oh." With that one word and that fleeting look of suspicion, she is, for a moment, almost the twin of her brother. "What are you doing here?"

"Rennie's here to see me." The old man crows the words with immense satisfaction. "Make us some coffee, will you, Katya?"

"Grandpa, I don't think it's a good idea—"

"Coffee, Katya," he says.

She smiles tightly, trying to hide her displeasure.

"A whole year she's been gone," he says to me before she's even out of the room. "Got a scholarship to some fancy school back east and never came to visit until now. The next thing I know, she's ordering me around—this is good for you, Grandpa, this is no good for you, do this, don't do that." He raises his voice to make sure she hears what he says next. "A person who really cared about her grandfather wouldn't have left in the first place. And she would have called more often. And visited!"

Katya sighs. "Coffee it is," she says and closes the door softly.

Curtis putters around the small room, clearing off a couple of chairs while he leans heavily on his walker. I lift stacks of books for him and set them on the floor. Finally, he sinks onto one chair and waves me into the other.

"I didn't think you'd come back," he says.

"I wanted to ask you about Mirella."

He smiles. "Lovely Mirella. I thought about her all night. There are plenty of things I don't remember, but I do remember her. She was beautiful. Long black hair, big brown eyes. Spectacular figure. I suppose she wouldn't look anything like that now though."

"I really need to find her," I say.

Curtis's bushy old-man eyebrows creep up his papery forehead.

"It's a long story," I tell him. "But I think she might know something important. You said she came here to get a job. Do you know if she worked in one of the car factories?"

The old man's eyes drift into the past. "If she did," he says, "the union would know. The UAW. I suppose you could ask them." He goes still. "Or I could." His eyes meet mine. "You want me to do that? I know some people. My son, Gerry, he used to work at GM before they shut the place down."

"I'd appreciate it," I say. My heart has sped up in my chest. He's right: If Mirella worked at a car plant, she would have been in the union. They must have some record of her. Maybe they even know where she is.

Curtis picks up the bell and rings it again, more vigorously this time.

A harried Katya appears at the door.

"Get me a phone," Curtis tells her.

She snaps off a salute. "Aye aye, captain."

"What's so important about Mirella?" Curtis asks while we wait.

I hesitate, thinking again how Adam warned me not to say anything about what we were doing. But this old man is ready to do me a favor.

"If she's the Mirella I'm looking for, she might have known someone that I'm trying to find out about."

"Oh?" He leans forward, waiting for me to continue.

I glance around the room at all the stuff that's crammed into it. At all the books and pictures and weapons and military memorabilia. I know nothing at all about Heinrich Franken besides the uniform he used to wear. Was he just an anonymous foot soldier? Or was he someone important? Someone who had something the Americans wanted?

I remember what Katya said last night about her grandfather: He knows everything there is to know about the Germans and World War II. Well, let's just see.

"I think Mirella was married to a man named Heinrich Franken."

"Franken?" The old man looks away, frowning. "Heinrich Franken, you say?"

"Who's Heinrich Franken?" It's Katya, back with a tray. On it are two mugs of coffee and a cordless phone. She sets the tray down on a spot Curtis has quickly cleared.

"Someone Rennie here is interested in."

Katya looks sharply at me. "Oh? And why is that?"

I shrug. I wish she would go away, but she doesn't. Instead, she turns to her grandfather.

"Do you know this person, Grandpa?"

"It's not a name I'm familiar with." Curtis reaches for his coffee, takes a sip and sinks back in his chair. "Thank you, Katya. If I need anything else, I'll ring the bell. Just like you told me to."

Katya isn't good at hiding her irritation. She doesn't like being dismissed, especially in front of someone who kicked down her front door last night. But she leaves us alone.

Curtis takes another sip of his coffee and reaches for the cordless phone. He frowns for a moment, then shakes his head.

"I don't recall Mirella mentioning the name Franken," he says. "She had a Spanish name. I'm sure of it."

"I need to know if she's the Mirella I'm looking for. If she is, I need to talk to her."

"Are you going to tell me why?"

I hesitate. "It's personal. But if I'm right and you help me, I promise to tell you everything."

"And if you're wrong?"

"Well, I guess then I'll feel like an idiot, and I'll probably just want to forget the whole thing."

The old man takes another sip of coffee.

"There's a book on the bedside table," he says.

I get up and go to the nightstand. There's a small book on it—an address book. There's also a clock radio and a pile of grenades. Seriously.

"These aren't live, are they?" I ask.

Curtis just chuckles.

I pick up the address book and hand it to him. He thumbs through it, finds what he's looking for and punches a number into the phone. Right away he's talking to someone, asking about Mirella, debating with whoever he's talking to whether she might have been in the union and what her last name might be. I should have asked that woman in Buenos Aires

"Gutierrez. Mirella Gutierrez," he says after a few moments. He's nodding. "Yeah, that sounds right. I'd appreciate it if you could look it up for me." He winks at me.

I take a sip of coffee even though my stomach is churning. What if Mirella is not only still alive, but lives right here in Detroit? What if she can tell me everything that I need to know? Could it be that easy?

I wait. Curtis waits. We look at each other. A minute ticks by. Then another. Curtis perks up.

"Yes? Uh-huh. Okay. Oh?" Is it my imagination, or is that disappointment I see on his face? "Sure. Talk to you later, Donnie."

He sets down the phone. "He's going to see what he can find. He says he'll get back to me later in the day."

Later in the day? What am I supposed to do until then?

"This fellow Franken you think she was married to. What's so special about him?"

I'm not supposed to tell. But the old man is helping me out. And if you want my opinion, he's enjoying himself or at least he's enjoying my company. I wonder how long it's been since he's had visitors. There are no next-door neighbors to drop by, that's for sure.

"I think maybe he was a Nazi," I say.

Curtis leans forward.

"When you say Nazi, do you mean those fellows who go around making a big fuss about white power? Or do you mean one of *those* guys?" He nods at something across the room. There's not as much light as there could be in this cluttered room, so it takes me a second to focus. When I see what he's looking at, I stand up.

"Is that…?" I walk to the far end of the room. In between a couple of bookshelves, under a display case of medals half hidden by a trunk, there's a framed black-and-white photograph. A big one, in a heavy, old frame. I can only see the top half of the face, but I recognize it for sure. "Is that who I think it is?"

"The old man himself," Curtis says. "Signed by him too."

I reach for the frame. My hand stops an inch short, and I glance over my shoulder. "Can I take a closer look?"

"Knock yourself out." Curtis is grinning, pleased that I'm admiring—if that's the right word—this treasure of his.

One of my hands grips the frame, and I start to lift it. But it and the glass are heavier than they look. I need two hands. I lift the picture until the whole face is visible, along with the scrawling signature underneath. It's him, all right. *Der Führer*. Adolf Hitler. And, sure enough, he's signed the photo: *Für meinen lieben Fritz*.

"This must be worth a lot," I say, although I wonder who in their right mind would want to hang this guy on their wall.

"I'm sure Gerry will find out exactly how much after I'm gone," the old man says. "He's been eyeing it. On the one hand, he calls my stuff junk." I can't tell if this bothers him. "On the other, he knows that one man's junk is another man's treasure."

I return the photo to its place so that only the eyes are visible. Now that I know whose eyes they are, it feels kind of creepy to have them on me.

"This Franken. Are you saying he was one of those Nazis?" Curtis asks.

"Yeah. I'm pretty sure."

"What else do you know about him?"

"Not much. Just the name. And that he lived in Argentina for a while."

"Argentina, huh? Well, he wasn't the only one, I guess. A lot of Nazis fled to South America— Argentina, Brazil, Paraguay, Chile." He shakes his head. "Franken. It's not much to go on."

He peers around the room. So do I. That's when I see the window at the back of the room. I didn't notice it last night, but the sun is doing its best to filter through layers of grime, and I can make out the backyard. It isn't much. An expanse of snow. A sagging chicken-wire fence. A garage at the end of an uncleared driveway, with a shed to one side.

"If this Franken fellow has a story to tell, then I'll probably have it here somewhere," Curtis says. "Come back later. Come for supper. If nothing else, Donnie will have got back to me by then."

I think of Katya and the way she looks at me, like I'm dog dirt she just stepped in. I doubt she'll welcome me at the family dinner table.

"Are you sure? Your family—"

"It's my house. I'm sure. Come by around six. I'll see what I have by then."

I say okay. How can I refuse? Curtis is the best lead I have.

I'm on the porch, having miraculously avoided both Katya—she must be out or somewhere else in the house—and Eric. I shut the front door behind me, stride down the walk and am heading past the driveway when I see someone skulking at the end of the driveway. A big guy, in jeans and boots and a puffy parka, a tuque on his head. He's peeking through the window in the small side door to the garage, his hands cupped around his eyes so that he can see inside. He tries the knob. It doesn't give. He glances around. I keep walking but double back quickly. There's something furtive about the guy. When I see him again, he's jimmying the door with something. He's breaking into the garage—in broad daylight. Geez, this is some town.

I tell myself it's none of my business. But I'm witnessing a crime. I should do something—go back to the house, maybe, and tell someone. At the very least, I should check out the situation. Maybe that will scare off the guy.

I stroll down the driveway to the garage. The small side door is closed now, but just barely. I see light dancing around inside. The guy must have a flashlight. I nudge the door open. The guy in the puffy parka is there. He's caught something in the beam of a small pocket flashlight. Something up in a storage space below the roof. He reaches up. He's trying to get his hands around it. A wooden box.

"Hey!" I say.

The guy whirls around. His whole body is tense. He's gone into a fighter's crouch, and it hits me—I'm not back home in Canada, I'm here in Detroit, Michigan, home of the concealed weapon. Maybe this isn't such a good idea.

But the guy doesn't do what I'm all of a sudden afraid he's going to do. He doesn't pull a gun on me. He doesn't fly at me, either, fists ready to do damage. Instead, he says, "Get out of here if you know what's good for you."

"As far as I know, this isn't your garage," I say.

"It isn't yours either." His head is cocked to one side, and his eyes are searching me all over. "You're not even from around here. You're from north of the border, right? Does your mama know you're down here?"

Right. The old best-defense-is-a-good-offense defense. And while he's using it on me, he's pushed the box back away from the edge of the storage space, and he's reaching for something else.

"Maybe I should call the cops," I say, mostly to see what reaction I get. From what I've heard, the cops are about as likely to show up for a reported prowler in a garage as the fire department is for a lit cigarette.

I watch the guy's hand close around something. He pulls it down; it's a snow shovel. He hefts it and pushes by me. I follow him outside, and we both stop short. Eric is standing there, minus his jacket. He's scowling.

"What's going on?" he wants to know.

Puffy Jacket holds up the shovel. "I went to get the shovel so I could clear the driveway, and I found him inside." He jerks his head in my direction.

Eric's eyes light on me. His mouth is a hard, straight, lipless line. He's waiting for an explanation, which tells me he's more than willing to believe Puffy Jacket. The two of them clearly know each other.

They say honesty is the best policy. I decide to see if *they* know what they're talking about.

"I saw this guy"—I jerk my head at Puffy—"lurking around your garage."

"Lurking?" Puffy snorts. "Listen to this guy. Lurking!"

Eric is listening—intently—so I continue.

"That's what it looked like to me. So I went to check it out."

"And?" Eric demands.

That puts Puffy's nose out of joint. "A guy does another guy a favor, and this is what happens? Fine." He thrusts the snow shovel at Eric. "You want to give me the third degree over nothing, you can clear your own driveway!" He jams his hands in his pockets and marches away. Eric doesn't even turn his head. He's focused on me.

"What was he doing in there?"

"Looking for something." I glance at Puffy's back. He's made it to the road and is booting it down the street. He is not a happy camper. "Maybe the snow shovel."

"Yeah?" Eric looks at the tool that's now in his hand. "I was looking for this earlier. Thought I was going to have to buy a new one. Where did he find it?"

I tell him. I don't mention the box, because now that I know Puffy and Eric know each other well enough for Eric to take it as a given that Puffy would want to clear the driveway, I think maybe what happened in there is none of my business.

"See you," I say.

"Not if I see you first."

When I turn to go, Eric is holding the snow shovel. When I look back from the street, he's out of sight. The side door to the garage is still open.

SEVEN

I have a lot of time to kill until six o'clock tonight. First on my order of business, I need a place for the night. I walk downtown, spot a Holiday Inn almost instantly and go inside. The clerk at the desk, a squeaky-clean type in a white shirt and tie and a gray jacket with a name tag pinned to the lapel—Thomas Hadley—looks me over. Maybe I imagine the slight curl of distaste his lips make, but I'm pretty sure I don't. I'm wearing a too-thin leather jacket, faded jeans and troublemaker boots, and I'm not carrying any luggage.

"May I help you?" he says after he's finished his none-too-subtle inspection.

"I'd like a room."

His eyes rake over me again, and I'm torn between wishing I'd doubled back to the diner Jacques works at to pick up my duffel and wanting to pound some respect into Thomas Hadley. I mean, how does he know I'm not some millionaire's son?

"Do you have a reservation?" he asks.

"No. But I bet you have a few vacancies."

He fiddles with his computer for a few minutes, probably just to make me sweat.

"We require a credit-card imprint," he says finally, as if that will settle the matter and send me on my way.

I dig the Major's gold card out of my wallet and slap it down on the counter.

Hadley looks at it. Then looks up. "And valid photo ID."

Out comes the wallet again. I toss my driver's license onto the counter next to the credit card.

Hadley picks it up gingerly—you know, in case it's smeared all over with some homeless person/petty criminal contagious disease. He examines the photo on the license and compares it to the face in front of him.

"Your name?" he asks, like it's some kind of trick question.

I tell him.

"Address?" He holds the license so I can't see it. He's still trying to trip me up.

I rattle off my address and throw in my birth date just to hurry things along. Hadley looks disappointed.

"And how long will you be staying with us, Mister…Charbonneau?" he asks. He mispronounces my name.

"One night. Maybe two."

He begins entering information into the computer in front of him. It takes a few minutes, but he finally gets my signature and slips me a key card. He even manages to thank me for choosing Holiday Inn without choking on the words. Jerk.

The first thing I notice when I get up to the room is how warm it is. In fact, it's the toastiest I've been since leaving Uruguay. The second thing is how comfortable the bed is. I spread-eagle on it like a kid about to make a snow angel. I think about texting Adam to see how he's doing, but I'm pretty sure that whatever he's up to, I'm going to feel bad because, so far, I've got nothing useful. I haven't found Mirella—although it's possible, I guess, that the union will have a record of her—and I know nothing more about the Nazi in the newspaper clipping, other than a name that has a pretty good chance of turning out to be fake. As for my grandfather, it's still a complete mystery why he was masquerading as someone named Klaus Adler. I decide to wait. I'll contact Adam when I have something concrete to report.

I close my eyes. When I open them again, I jump, thinking someone must have snuck into the room—Hadley?—and closed all the blinds. It's so dark.

But the blinds are open, and I realize with a jolt that I've slept the day away. It's nearly six, and the sun is down for the night.

I scramble to my feet and sniff my armpits. I could use a shower, but I have no clean clothes to change into. Everything is in my duffel bag. Still…

I strip down and shower fast. I wash the underarms of my shirt and blow-dry them. I don't have any deodorant, but at least I smell like soap now and not a bad case of BO. I dress and then I'm off to the old man's place, feeling less than hopeful that he's managed to come up with something.

I ring the bell.

No answer.

The front of the house is dark. There's no light in the hall, none in the living room, none in the front upstairs windows.

I circle around to the back to see if there's any sign of life there.

A light is shining out of the old man's window, so I go up onto the porch to take a look, to see if he's in there.

He isn't. Who I see instead is Katya.

She's alone in Curtis's room. She's moving things—piles of books, boxes, stacks of paper—holding them up and then putting them back down again after she's given them a thorough once-over. She's doing it methodically, moving slowly around the room. After a minute or two, she stands up straight and shakes her head. She's looking for something, I'm sure of it. But what?

She goes over to the trunk, the one in front of the massive picture of *Der Führer*. She tries to lift the lid, but it doesn't give. She tries again. Nothing. She kneels down in front of it for a better look. My guess: the trunk is locked. She stands up, hands on her hips.

For a few seconds, she's like a statue. Then she tries to move the trunk, pull it forward, which I don't understand. Moving it isn't going to make it open.

From the effort she puts into it, it's clear that the trunk is heavy. When she straightens up again, her shoulders are heaving, as if she's breathing hard. Then she reaches over the trunk, grabs hold of the framed Adolf and starts to lift it.

Which is when someone shouts.

I hear a thump and a curse. It's coming from outside Curtis's bedroom door, and my eyes shift there. There's a chair in front of the door. That's funny, I think, until I realize that Katya has put it there to warn her when someone tries to come in. She starts to put the picture back, but it slips from her hands. There's a crash, followed by another muffled shout from the other side of the door:

"What's going on in there?"

Katya freezes. She stands there for a long time, staring down at what she's done. At least, that's what I think at the time. Someone hammers on the door. *Bang, bang, bang, bang, bang.* Katya swings into action, putting everything she's got into pushing the trunk back into place. She rushes over to the door and yanks the chair aside. The old man shuffles in at double time, pushing his walker in front of him. He's in a robe, there's a towel over one shoulder, and his hair is sticking up in all directions. He cleaned up, same as me.

"Why was my door locked?" he demands.

"It wasn't locked, Grandpa. I was just tidying up. I guess I moved the chair in front of the door without noticing it. I'm sorry. How was your shower?"

But he doesn't want to talk about his shower. He wants to know what that crash was.

Katya is all innocence. "That was just the door hitting the chair."

I pull away from the window and circle around to the front of the house again. This time I ring twice. I also *rat-a-tat-tat* on the door to make sure someone hears me.

It's Katya who answers. Her cheeks are flushed.

"What are you doing here?"

"Your grandfather invited me to dinner."

She scowls.

"You can ask him," I say cheerily.

She's itching to close the door on me, but the old man's walker swings into view, followed by the old man. He's still wearing his bathrobe, but it's open now, and I see he's managed to get himself into a pair of clean pants.

"Come in. Come in." He smiles at me but shoots a look of irritation at Katya.

I step inside and remove my boots.

"Don't you have to check on dinner?" Curtis says to Katya.

For a second, it's hard to tell who she's angrier at, me or her grandfather. She spins around and marches to the back of the house, where, I have to say, something smells delicious.

"Follow me," Curtis says.

I pad down the hall behind him to his room. The trunk is back in its place in front of Hitler, and any damage Katya did to the frame or the glass when she dropped it isn't visible. I think about telling the old man what I saw, but how would that make me look, peeking into his room like a burglar on the prowl? I tell myself that Katya's business has nothing to do with me.

"Did you find out anything?" I ask.

Curtis has pushed his way over to the closet. He opens the door and stares inside before pulling out a clean shirt. He shrugs off his bathrobe, and I see how skinny he is—all bone and wrinkly skin. He's unsteady on his feet when he lets go of his walker, so I watch him closely, ready to prop him up if I have to. He gets one arm in a sleeve no problem, but then he has to hunt around for the other arm, which isn't easy because the shirt is hanging half off him and the empty sleeve is behind his back. He keeps working at it silently until I can't stand it anymore. I grab the sleeve, even though he growls that he doesn't need help. When he doesn't thank me, I get the feeling I've insulted him.

Finally, he drops into a chair.

"Did that union guy get back to you?" I ask.

"Donnie? Yes, he did."

I wait.

"And?" I ask finally, exasperated.

"Mirella worked at a Chrysler plant until she retired out of there."

I hold my breath.

"She was active in the union too."

Was, as in before she retired?

"She died back in the nineties. No husband. No kids."

Well, that's that. Mirella isn't going to be able to help me. I'm exactly nowhere. I've made no progress at all.

"What about Franken?" I ask.

Curtis shoots me a sly smile. "I did some work for you, finding out about Mirella, and you still haven't told me why you want to talk to her. Anything else I do for you is going to be a trade—you want to get information, you have to give information."

"Does that mean you found out something about Heinrich Franken?"

"You want to get, you have to give," Curtis says.

I don't want to explain the whole mess, but I don't see I have much choice. Besides, whatever happened was so long ago now that the only people it probably matters to are me and my cousins. Even if my grandfather was a spy or a Nazi or whatever, what difference does it make now?

The doorbell rings.

"Can somebody get that?" Katya shouts from the kitchen.

I look at the old man.

"Gerry's out," he says. "Eric too, I think."

What else can I do? "I'll go."

The bell rings again. I step out into the hall. Katya appears in the doorway to the kitchen, wiping her hands on an apron and looking annoyed, as if everything always falls to her. Maybe it does. Maybe that's why she left home.

"I got it," I yell.

"It's probably Uncle Gerry. He goes out for a few beers with his friends and then can't find his keys when they drop him back home." She goes back into the kitchen.

I head in the other direction, to answer the door.

It's a sharp-looking guy—overcoat, scarf, leather gloves, a gift-bagged bottle in one hand and a bunch of flowers in the other.

"You must be Eric," he says, grinning and shifting the gift bag to the hand that's holding the flowers. "I'm Noah. It's great to finally meet you." He pumps my hand and looks as happy as a kid who's just met his all-time-favorite superhero.

"Who is it?" Katya calls from the kitchen.

Noah smiles at the sound of her voice and steps forward to come inside. The only problem is, I don't shift to give him the room. It's not my house, and he may be Noah, but I don't know him from Adam.

I call back to Katya. "Some guy says his name is Noah."

Katya must have a Star Trek transporter back there in the kitchen, because she's at my elbow in a nano-second. She shoves me aside.

"Noah, what are you doing here?"

Her tone, a mix of stunned and angry, wipes the smile right off his face.

"Aren't you happy to see me?" His mouth turns down into a sad-puppy pout.

Katya glances at me. She pushes Noah out onto the porch, steps outside with him and closes the door. She's in a sweater and leggings, with a chef's apron overtop. If she wants to freeze out there, what do I care? And boy, is she ever annoyed with Noah. I can hear her right through the door, mostly because Gerry didn't do a great job replacing the part of the doorframe that I broke. There's a gap between it and the side of the door.

"It's about time I met your family." That's Noah, sounding reasonable and also a little hurt.

"I told you I'd handle it. I don't think it's a good idea for you to be here." That's Katya.

"They have to meet me sooner or later."

"That's not what I'm here for, and you know it."

There's a long pause, and I'm ready to head back to the old man when I hear Noah again. He says, "Did you find it?"

Katya answers, but she lowers her voice so that all I hear is a low hum. Noah matches his voice to hers. Normally, I wouldn't care. But there was Katya in the old man's room, clearly looking for something that, as far as I can make out, she didn't find. And the next thing I know, here's a guy named Noah who wants to know if she found it. It makes a guy wonder: found what? I also wonder why Katya doesn't want Noah here—and why he showed up, apparently unexpected.

When I get back to Curtis's room, he's scrambling around in a drawer, pulling stuff out—batteries and coins, bits of paper, pill bottles, paper clips, what I think is a tie clip, some cufflinks, more scraps of paper.

"Did you lose something?" I ask.

"Aha!" Triumphant, he holds up something. A key.

"Come on," he says. "Let's go get a nip."

He pushes his walker out into the hallway, waits until I'm standing beside him and then locks the door.

He drops the key into his pants pocket and is off to the living room.

We're intercepted on the way when the front door opens and Gerry bursts in. His face is red, his nose is redder, and he's stomping his feet.

"Getting colder out there."

"You're just in time for a nip," Curtis says.

The door opens again. This time it's Katya and Noah. Katya is wearing Noah's overcoat. Noah is shivering in a sharp-looking black suit.

"Grandpa, Uncle Gerry, this is Noah. He's staying for dinner."

The two men look at the newcomer. The puzzled expressions on their faces make me think that not only have they never met Noah, but they've never even heard of him.

"I—I met him at school," Katya says.

Noah nudges her. "There's more to it than that." He smiles at her and holds out a hand. Shyly, Katya takes it.

"We're engaged," she says softly.

"Engaged?" Gerry shouts the word, as if she's just announced that she's been arrested for solicitation. "Engaged?"

"I love your niece, sir." Noah gazes lovingly at Katya. "She's the best thing that ever happened to me."

Gerry ignores him. "How can you be engaged to someone I've never heard of?" he demands. "When you were here at Thanksgiving, you didn't mention him. And now you're telling me you're getting married? I don't know the first thing about him."

Katya's cheeks flush. She slips out of Noah's coat and drapes it on the banister. "We can talk about this later, Uncle Gerry. I'm in the middle of making dinner." She turns to Noah. "I could use an extra pair of hands."

But Gerry is blocking the way. "We'll talk about it now."

"Uncle Gerry—"

"I've been responsible for you and your brother since your mother died. I raised you. Me. Not that good-for-nothing father of yours."

"Gerry." It's the old man. He touches Gerry's arm—a warning. Gerry shakes him off.

"I raised you, and I want to make sure you're doing the right thing. You're nineteen, Katya. You're too young to get married."

"Mom got married when she was eighteen."

"Yeah, and look how that worked out. What do you even know about this guy?"

Noah stiffens. A sharp look crosses his face. Katya catches it.

"Uncle Gerry, Noah is standing right here. Don't talk about him as if he isn't." Her face softens, and she comes in close to her uncle. "I love him and he loves me. What do you want to know?"

"For one thing, what he does for a living."

"I just graduated from law school," Noah says. "I'm about to start an articling position."

"In other words, you're unemployed." Gerry, unemployed himself, is not impressed.

"He has an articling position, Uncle Gerry. And great prospects. Noah graduated at the top of his class."

"When did you meet him? Why didn't you mention him before?"

"We met two months ago—"

"Two months! What can you possibly know about a person in two months?"

"—and I didn't mention him at Thanksgiving because I wanted to be sure."

"And now you are?" Gerry throws up his arms in disbelief.

"We both are," Noah says calmly.

Gerry shoots him a who-asked-you look. "It's too soon. You don't know him well enough to marry him. You're far too young to even *think* about marriage."

Katya has an answer to that. "We're not planning to get married until Noah passes the bar. That will give us plenty of time. It will give *you* plenty of time, Uncle Gerry." She goes up on tiptoe and plants a kiss on her uncle's cheek. Gerry's whole body relaxes a couple of degrees. "Give us a chance, Uncle Gerry. Once you get to know Noah, you'll like him. I promise."

Gerry looks far from convinced. He turns his back on Noah. "I'm going to go and get cleaned up."

"Dinner is in fifteen minutes," Katya tells him.

"Don't forget to set an extra place for Rennie," Curtis says, and just like that, the two of us are on everyone's radar. Curtis introduces himself and me to Noah. Gerry glowers at me, but that's nothing compared to the look Katya gives me. Now that her beloved is here, it's clear she wants me gone. And, honestly, I'd be glad to oblige. But I haven't figured out yet if Curtis knows something about Franken or if he's playing with me. If I can get him to tell me what, if anything, he's found out before supper is on the table, I'll be glad to go. But he's got his mind fixed on a nip. He offers one to Noah, who accepts, and shoots off to the living room, making remarkably good time with his walker. I try a couple of times to get his attention, but once he's had one nip, he wants another. Plus he's grilling Noah and succeeding in making him squirm—although if you ask me, it's more out of irritation than nervousness.

Finally, I get a break. Noah excuses himself and heads for the kitchen and Katya. I lean into the old man to ask again about Franken. Eric chooses that exact time to show up with Puffy Jacket in tow.

"Just the guy I've been looking for," Eric says to me.

"Yeah? What for?"

Katya calls everyone to supper. Eric catches sight of Noah.

"Who's that?" he asks his sister.

Katya notices Puffy. "He has to leave," she says, doing to him exactly what she complained her uncle did to Noah.

"He's staying," Eric says. He's staring at Noah, plainly curious. Katya slams down another place setting, and we all sit.

EIGHT

The meal gets off to a bad start when Gerry, more out of sorts now than he was when he met Noah, ignores the food on his plate and says, "Noah what?"

"I beg your pardon, sir?" Noah is on his best behavior, but the respectful "sir" does nothing to placate Gerry.

"Noah's your first name. What's your last name?"

"Green."

At the end of the table, Eric is talking low to Puffy Jacket.

Silence from Gerry. Then: "Is that the original name, or did your people change it?"

"Sir?"

"Uncle Gerry—"

Gerry's face is all innocence when he looks at Katya and says, "I'm just asking." But his eyes go hard when they skip back to Noah.

"I'm not sure I follow you, sir," Noah says. There's tension in his voice.

Katya, sitting opposite him, reaches for his hand.

"Noah. That's a biblical name. Old Testament," Gerry says.

"Genesis," Noah agrees.

"In other words, not New Testament," Gerry says.

Noah agrees again. "It's not Matthew, Mark, Luke or John."

"So I'm wondering about your last name, Green. Was it something else originally?"

"You mean, like Greenblatt or Greenberg, something like that?" Noah is still smiling, but his smile isn't reflected in his eyes.

"Noah, this isn't the time—" Katya begins.

Noah shakes off her hand. "Your uncle asked me a question. I have no problem answering it." He turns back to Gerry. "It was Grunberg. My grandfather changed it when he immigrated here. I think he felt it would be better."

"Better for who?" Gerry asks. "If you ask me, people who change their names have something to hide."

"That may be true." Noah sounds calm, maybe too calm, considering Gerry's accusing tone. "But in my grandfather's case, he changed his name to avoid the prejudice he suffered before and during the war. What about *your* grandfather?"

This gets Eric's attention. He stares at his uncle.

"Noah, please!"

"What are you talking about?" Gerry thunders. "What are you saying?"

"It's just a question, sir."

Katya squeezes his hand. Her eyes are pleading.

"My grandfather came here right after World War Two, as soon as he was strong enough to travel," Noah says.

"Strong enough?" Eric perks up. "He was wounded?"

"He was from Poland."

Eric says nothing, waiting for more information, I think.

"He's lucky he survived," Noah says. "No one else in his family did."

"What do you mean?" Eric asks.

"He was in a concentration camp."

"Yeah? And he made it out? That's something, huh?" Eric is impressed.

"I guess you could call it an accomplishment," Noah says. "He was lucky. The guy in charge of the camp was one of those sadistic guys you hear about. A guy named Waldmann." He turns to the old man, who is sitting at the end of the table. "Katya tells me you're a real expert on the Nazis. She says your father was in that war. Did you ever come across the name Waldmann?"

The old man's hand is clamped around his glass. He's coming down to the bottom of his second nip, which is a pretty big one.

"Can't say that I know the name." He lifts the glass, thinks a moment and then shakes his head. "No, I don't know that name."

Noah glances at Katya. His smile is gentle, loving.

"Well, your grandfather may know a lot about the war, but he's hardly the expert you make him out to be, Katya." He says it casually, like it's no big deal, but the old man stiffens as if he's been slapped.

"I'm more of an expert than you'll ever be, young man," he says.

Noah shakes his head slowly. "I don't think so." He is respectful, as if he wants to make sure everyone understands that he's not being critical. "An expert, someone who really knows the war and the National Socialist Party, would know that name. The man was notorious."

"And I suppose *you're* an expert?" The old man is taking it badly.

"Me? No. But my grandfather—now there was someone who knew everything there is to know. You could say he made it his business to know. His wife, my grandmother, was American. She didn't go through what he went through. She tried to understand. But how can anyone understand something so incomprehensible?" He looks fondly across the table at Katya. "My grandfather worked in the garment industry when he immigrated here. He was a tailor. Men's suits. But his whole life, his life outside of working and providing for his family, was all about the past, about what happened to him and his family, why it happened, who was responsible. He couldn't let it go."

The old man drains his glass and holds it up.
Katya shakes her head. The old man thrusts the
glass at her. She gets up and refills it, but only half
an inch.

"He's sure he saw him once," Noah says.

"Saw who?" Eric asks.

"Waldmann."

"The guy who ran the concentration camp? Your
grandfather saw him? Where?"

"For the love of Mike!" Gerry slams a fist onto
the table, and all the glasses jump in response. "We're
eating dinner. You're a guest here. Why are we talking
about this?"

"I'm sorry, sir." Noah squeezes Katya's hand.
"Sorry, Katya."

"It's okay."

"It's *not* okay."

Gerry gets up and disappears into the living room.
I look around the table. Eric is frowning at me as if
I'm the problem. The old man is frowning too, but
at his plate, not at anyone in particular. Puffy Jacket
is eating. He's the only person who is. Gerry returns
to the table with a glass of something—I'm guessing

Scotch or bourbon. Katya shoots him a warning look. He sees it and glowers at her. I wish I was out of here.

The meal goes on in strained silence until, finally, Katya says, "We were thinking—Noah and I were thinking—" She looks across the table and Noah nods, encouraging her. "We're going to have an extra room, and we thought it would be nice if Eric came and lived with us."

"What?" This seems to be news to Eric.

"What?" It's definitely news to Gerry.

"You'd like Boston, Eric," Katya says. "It's not like here. It's nice. You could get your GED and maybe think about college."

Eric shakes his head. "I'm done with school."

"You need an education to get anywhere these days," Gerry says.

"I'm eighteen. I can look after myself."

"Then why are you mooching off me? Why don't you have a job?"

"Uncle Gerry, please!" I'm guessing this isn't the way Katya envisioned dinner. She turns pleading eyes on Eric.

"You could make new friends."

"I already have friends."

"You'll have more opportunities there. You could get a part-time job while you finish—"

"I'm not going back to school!"

"And he's not going to Boston," Gerry says. "He's my responsibility. He goes where I say he goes. And I say he stays right here."

"Hey!" Eric stiffens in his chair. "Nobody tells me what to do."

"I'm not telling. I'm asking," Katya says with a pointed look at her uncle. "At least come for a while, Ricky." I guess that's her pet name for him, and it changes the look on his face. His dark eyes go soft. Whatever else Eric is, he's also a guy who cares about his sister.

"I don't know, Katty."

"Think about it? That's all I'm asking. You can put all that trouble behind you—"

"He's not in trouble," Gerry says. "In case you haven't noticed, the cops have nothing except their suspicions. Their *unfounded* suspicions."

It doesn't surprise me that Eric's been in trouble with the cops. I wonder what he's done.

Katya ignores him. "You can start fresh, Ricky. Just think about it. And if you come, it's not like it's a lifelong commitment. *I'm* not going to nail you down. If you don't like it, you can always leave. Just promise me you'll think about it."

Eric nods. "Okay."

The room falls silent again. People still aren't eating. Katya looks at Noah. There are tears in her eyes. Noah squeezes her hand.

"I guess this is as good a time as any," he says.

Everyone stares at him. They're probably wondering the same thing I am—a good time for what?

"Katya and I are inviting the family to dinner tomorrow night. To celebrate our engagement."

Gerry downs whatever is in his glass.

Curtis glowers at Noah.

"You all have to come," Katya says. "The whole reason I came back here is so that you can get to know Noah."

I know that's not true. I saw the surprise on her face when Noah showed up. She wasn't expecting him. He's not the reason she's here.

"Sounds to me like you came back here to steal Eric," Gerry grumbles.

Another squeeze of Noah's hand seems to stiffen Katya's resolve. She smiles, even though her lips are trembling.

"You all have to come. No excuses." She turns her blue eyes on her uncle. "Please, Uncle Gerry? It would mean so much to me to have you there. You raised me. Me and Ricky both."

Gerry's tight, angry mouth relaxes. It's no mystery what his Achilles heel is. I wonder what life was like in this house back when Gerry was still working a good job in an auto factory. There would have been plenty of money to go around then and fewer worries to plague everyone. They would have had neighbors. And streetlights. A normal life. All the things that are next to impossible when no one has a job and everyone has given up on life because it looks like life has given up on them.

"I guess I can make the time," he says.

Katya gets up and goes to the end of the table. She wraps her arms around Gerry's neck and kisses him on the cheek.

"Thank you, Uncle Gerry." She ventures a smile. "And you'll walk me down the aisle when the time comes, won't you?"

Gerry shifts awkwardly in his chair. "If you want me to."

"I do."

"And this dinner thing," Gerry says, "We'll all be there, right, Dad? Eric?"

"I have plans," Eric says.

"Change them. This is important to your sister."

Eric shoots his uncle a look of irritation. Then his eyes meet Katya's, and he melts just like his uncle.

"Okay. Fine."

Everyone, it seems, will do just about anything for Katya.

Eric crumples his napkin and throws it down. "Me and Duane gotta roll." Puffy Jacket, aka Duane, wipes his mouth on a paper napkin. Before Gerry or Katya can protest, Eric nods at me. "Him too."

I point to myself. *Me?*

"I got a line on a new fridge," Eric says.

"Are you crazy?" Gerry says. "We can't afford a new fridge."

Eric grins. "It's not gonna cost a thing except a little heavy lifting. A guy I know owes me. All we have to do is pick up the fridge and bring it here. Duane already volunteered to help. If Grandpa's friend will pitch in, it's ours."

"What about you?" Curtis says. "What are you going to do?"

"I'm going to drive the truck. I'd help to carry it, but ever since that little accident—"

"What accident?" I ask.

"The less said about that, the better," Gerry says. "It's free? No strings?"

"None."

"Okay. Go."

Eric and Duane stand up. Eric looks at me. "Well? My sister made you a nice dinner. That's not worth an hour of your time?"

I glance at Curtis. "We can talk when I get back, right?"

The old man nods.

Fine, I'll help move the fridge. It should be easy. Get it, bring it back, and then find out what, if anything, Curtis knows. What could go wrong?

The truck Eric borrows is a mostly rusted-out used-to-be-red pickup with a malfunctioning heater. We squeeze in, Eric behind the wheel, me in the middle, and Duane on the outside. Duane doesn't say a word. Eric doesn't talk much either. We drive for about twenty minutes through a maze of streets, most of them without working streetlights. I don't know the city, so I don't know what direction we're traveling in. I just know that by the time we get where we're going, my feet are freezing inside my boots, and I wish I had a thicker jacket. I also wish I had gloves. I should have bought some at the airport. I'm glad I have my head tucked up that stupid hat, even if it makes me look like a refugee from Santa's workshop.

Eric pulls to the curb in what was once a commercial area but where the storefronts are now mostly boarded over. The two that aren't—a 7-Eleven and a liquor store—have metal grates over the windows, and I don't think it's a stretch to imagine that the clerks have ready access to firearms. Eric jumps down from behind the wheel. Duane slides out the passenger side. We both wait for Eric's instructions.

"The fridge should be around the back," he says, pointing at what looks like a dark alley. "My buddy, he left it behind this store."

This store is an appliance store—new and used—that looks like it's closed down, although from the way Eric is talking, maybe it's just closed for the night or maybe for the holidays.

"You got a flashlight?" Duane asks.

"Check the glove compartment."

Duane does and comes up empty.

"It's a white fridge," Eric says impatiently. "It's not like it's invisible. Go and get it. I'll back the truck up."

Duane looks annoyed. He doesn't seem to want to be here any more than I do. I wonder what his relationship is to Eric. I also wonder where Skull is. Why didn't Eric ask him to help out?

"You coming?" Duane asks me.

I trot off after him. The trot turns into a slow, cautious walk as soon as we enter the alley. It's darker than dark in there. I can make out shapes, but I can't tell what they are.

"Maybe we should get him to shine the headlights down here," I say.

Duane doesn't seem interested in the idea.

"Let's just get this over with," he says. "I'm freezing."

Yeah, and he's wearing a puffy jacket. What does he think I am?

I stay close. We get to the end of the alley and look around. Sure enough, there's something big and white behind the appliance store, just like Eric said.

And when I say big, I mean big. I hope Eric measured it. I hope it's going to fit through his front door.

We start toward the fridge. Duane stands in front of it and is running his hands over it, maybe to get the size of it, when suddenly we're hit by a beam of light. My first thought is that Eric has done something helpful: he's turned the truck around and aimed the headlights down the alley so we can see what we're doing. But I realize right away that I've got it wrong, because the light is coming from the wrong direction.

Duane must realize something's off too, because he spins around. We both do. The light's in our faces. Duane raises one hand to shield his eyes. I hear a bang like a gunshot—except, I think of course it isn't. I squint to try to see past the light and think I see a couple of guys. One of them steps forward. He's wearing a long coat that reaches almost to his ankles and a black watch cap that hides his hair. But that's almost beside the point, because it's his face that draws me. I can't take my eyes off it. He's a white guy, I'm pretty sure of that, but he's got this giant tattoo that covers most of his face. It's a spider. A massive spider.

There's another bang. Like another gunshot.

Then a loud clang. It comes from overhead and sounds like a door closing. Maybe someone just came out onto the fire escape. I look up, but I don't see anyone on it.

Spider Face hears the clang too. He glances up. Then he shouts to me, "Hey!"

A beam of light illuminates something—a gun—sailing through the air at me. *Geez*. I catch it by reflex. I'm afraid if I don't and it hits the ground, it will go off and someone, maybe me, will get hurt.

The lights click off. I hear footsteps, running.

I look around to see what Duane makes of what just happened. But he isn't there. It takes a few seconds for me to realize that he hasn't taken off. He's down on the ground. He doesn't answer when I ask him what he's doing. I crouch. He's so still. I touch him. He doesn't move. I realize I'm still holding the gun, and I drop it and press my ear to Duane's mouth. He's not breathing—or if he is, I can't tell. I yell for Eric as I start CPR. I yell for him a couple of times, but he doesn't show up.

Duane still isn't moving. I'm pretty sure he's dead. I sit back on my heels and put a hand to the ground to steady myself. That's when I feel something warm and wet—and sticky. I bring my hand up to my face, but I still can't see what it is. It's too dark. But I know. Boy, do I know. It's blood.

Suddenly I'm shaking all over, but it's not from the cold. The bangs I heard, the ones that sounded like gunshots—that's exactly what they were. Spider Face shot Duane. I can't believe it. I was standing with Duane. I could have been hit too. I could be lying there instead of Duane—or beside him—not breathing. Dead in an alley in Detroit. Worse, with no one I care about having any idea where I am. As far as the Major is concerned, I'm safely back in Toronto with my grandmother. As far as my grandmother knows, I'm about to show up on her doorstep, relaxed (well, as relaxed as anyone can be after ten straight days with the Major) and tanned from a beach vacation in Uruguay.

I fumble for my cell phone and call 9-1-1. I report the shooting. When the operator asks for my location, I realize I have no idea where I am. I stumble back down the alley to the street. When I get there, I see headlights coming in my direction. I freeze. Is it Spider Face? Has he come back to finish the job?

But it's not him. It's Eric, in the truck. He pulls to a stop and jumps out.

"Where's the fridge?" he demands. "Where's Duane?"

"Where were you? You said you were going to back up. Where the hell were you?" My voice doesn't sound right. For one thing, it's hollow, like an echo. And shaky, like the rest of me. I want to drive my fist through something. I can't believe any of this.

"I went to gas up," Eric says. "Where's Duane? What happened? Wasn't the fridge there? Because if it wasn't—"

I'm looking around for a street sign. There isn't one.

"Where are we?" I ask Eric.

"What? What do you mean? We're here."

"Where's here? What street is this?"

He tells me. I tell the 9-1-1 operator.

"Who's that?" Eric wants to know. "Who are you talking to?"

"The cross street?" I say. "What's the nearest cross street?"

"What's going on?"

I scream the question at him. My fury stuns him. He answers. I tell the 9-1-1 operator. I also tell her the few store signs I can see. She tells me to stay put.

I feel sick when I shove the phone back into my pocket. I was right there. I was no more than two feet away from him. I could have been shot.

That's it. I double over and throw up Katya's dinner.

"What the...?" Eric says. He calls Duane's name.

"He's dead," I say.

"Dead? What do you mean, dead?"

"Someone shot him."

Eric laughs. He takes another look at me. The laugh dies in his throat.

"What are you talking about?" He looks at the alley. Then he starts toward it.

I grab him to hold him back.

"Where is he?" he demands.

"You can't go back there. Someone shot him. It's a crime scene. We have to stay here."

We stay. We stand and wait, and I get colder and colder, until my teeth are chattering. It doesn't occur to me to get into the truck. Anyway, the heater isn't working properly.

An ambulance arrives.

The cops arrive.

NINE

I'm covered in blood after my attempted CPR. I'm still shaking. The ambulance guys check me out. They wrap me in a blanket because I'm shaking so hard. They inspect me for wounds. They listen to my heart a couple of times. Apparently, it's racing. They tell me it's shock at what I've witnessed. Once they're satisfied I'm not hurt, they hand me over to the cops, who take me back to a police station, put me into a small room and tell me to take a seat, that someone will be with me shortly. If I'm suspected of anything or under arrest, no one bothers to tell me. I'm not worried—not yet anyway. I haven't done anything.

Besides, down here the cops have to tell you whether you're arrested or not. If they don't and the case goes to trial, it will get kicked because they didn't follow the rules. But they fingerprinted me, which I don't understand. Why the fingerprints if I'm not under arrest? I guess I could have said no. But, like I said, I haven't done anything. If you haven't broken any laws, you have no worries, right?

So I sit—or try to—and I wait. I'm as squirmy as an addict in need of a top-up. I still can't believe what happened. I don't want to believe it. I stand again, and I pace. I stop for a few seconds to look at the mirror on one wall. Of course, I know it's not really a mirror. It's a one-way window. Whoever is on the other side can see me, and that's all I can see too. Me. With blood on the front of my jacket. With a face that looks too white considering how much surf and sun I've had lately.

Me, pacing. Which makes me look guilty of something. But I can't stop. I don't even want to think about sitting still. I just want out.

The door opens and a massive black guy comes into the room. He tells me his name— Daniel Carver—and says he's a homicide detective.

He's wearing a dark suit with a shirt and tie, and he's carrying a file folder. He flashes me his badge and tells me to take a seat.

"I didn't do anything," I tell him. That doesn't sound right. I don't want him to get the wrong idea. "I mean, I tried CPR. But it was too late." There, that's better. Sort of.

"I said sit." He doesn't yell it at me. It sounds more like a guy giving a command to his dog. And like a good dog—or like someone who knows enough about cops to know it's not a good idea to annoy them, not when something this serious has happened—I sit. But one of my legs is jumping up and down like it's keeping time to music that no one can hear. Carver notices. He looks at it. I make it stop. Carver looks me in the eye. My leg starts to jump again.

"Rennie Charbonneau. That's your name?" He's got the deepest voice I've ever heard and a way of talking like I'm a piece of garbage he's about to ditch as soon as he can find out who tossed me in his path. He scares me more than the Major ever has, and that's rare. I don't get scared very often, and I sure don't get intimidated. Maybe it's shock, like the ambulance guy said. "That's a French name, right?"

I nod. "My dad's Quebecois." Will a Detroit cop know what that is? "He's from Quebec. It's in Canada."

"I know where Quebec is," Carver says mildly. He's looking at a page inside the file folder. "What's a Canadian boy from Quebec doing down here in Detroit over Christmas, Rennie?"

I start to relax, even though I know I probably shouldn't. Just because a cop—a homicide cop, at that—sounds friendly, it doesn't mean he is. More than likely he's trying to find out what I sound like and look like and how I act when I'm not being grilled and not spinning a web of lies. He's using psychology on me. I tell myself to relax. I remind myself of something I've heard the Major say before, which is that you might be able to put one over on a good investigator now and then, but unless you're a career criminal—a *successful* career criminal—you're basically a rookie up against someone who's seen and heard it all. Carver is doing his job here, the same job he's been doing for a couple of decades, judging by the look of him. Me—I'm just in a situation that I sincerely hope is temporary.

"I'm on my way home from a vacation with my dad," I say.

He glances up from the folder. "Oh? He's here with you?"

"No, sir."

He hears the "sir," and a wolflike smile appears on his face.

"You trying to snow me, Rennie?"

"No, sir."

His eyes lock onto mine. If I look hard enough, I can see his vision of my future in their black depths. I want to look away, but I know not to. If you don't look straight at the cops when they're talking to you, they start to think you're lying. And if you're lying, then you're probably guilty of something. But what I said is true. For once I'm not trying to snow anyone with the "sir." It's just that Carver reminds me of the Major, so the "sir" is an automatic reflex.

"My dad shipped out," I tell him. Then, before he can ask, I add, "He's with the military. He has an assignment overseas. Afghanistan."

"And you?"

"Me?"

"You haven't explained what you're doing in Detroit. It says here you're a Canadian citizen, residing in Canada. You have friends here?"

"No, sir."

He looks at the file folder again. "You told the officers on the scene that you had dinner with friends and that you were in the alley where the shooting occurred because you were doing a favor for one of those friends."

I feel my leg jump. I wish it wouldn't, but I can't stop it. I realize it looks like he's caught me in a lie. But it's not a lie. The fact is, I can barely remember what I told the two uniforms who questioned me at the scene. Mostly I was thinking how close I'd just come to being a corpse like Duane. If those cops were to walk into the room right now, I doubt I'd recognize them. There are only two faces burned into my brain, and believe me, I wish they weren't. They're Duane after he stopped breathing and the guy with the massive spider tattoo.

"They aren't really friends," I tell Carver. "I mean, I didn't know any of them until the day before yesterday. They're more like acquaintances."

Carver shakes his head. He's disappointed. "It's late, Rennie, and it's been a long day. Let's not play word games, okay?"

"I was just trying to clari—"

"How long have you known McLennan?"

"Who?" Who's McLennan? I've never heard the name before.

Carver lets out a long, heavy sigh, like, Please Lord, why do you keep sending me kids who think that playing dumb is their smartest move?

"Eric McLennan. You telling me you don't know him?"

"I didn't know his last name." I assumed it was Forrester. Looks like I'm wrong. And where is he anyway? I lost track of him when the cops showed up. Did they bring him in too?

"It's McLennan," Carver says, like he can't believe he has to tell me this. Like he thinks the only reason he has to is because I'm wasting his precious time by acting clueless. "How long have you known him?"

"I met him the day before yesterday."

"But you were doing him a favor. That's what you said, isn't it?"

"Well, yeah. But it's not what you think."

"You have no idea what I think, Rennie."

My leg jumps again. The thing is, I have a pretty good idea what's running through his mind. I've dealt with cops before. Plenty of times. But it was always for stupid stuff, never for anything this serious. Never for homicide. The stupid stuff I did, I could deal with that. And those cops didn't scare me because, seriously, what was the worst they could do? I live with the Major, after all, and there isn't a cop alive that can be harder on me than the Major is.

At least, there hasn't been until now.

I remind myself of some important facts. Fact one: I am old enough to be tried as an adult in any jurisdiction in North America. Fact two: homicide is as serious as it gets. Fact three: some states have the death penalty, and I'm not at all sure that Michigan isn't one of them.

Carver leans back in his chair. "Why don't you tell me exactly what happened tonight, Rennie?"

Finally, I have a chance to lay it out so that it makes sense.

I start by telling him that I had supper at Eric's house, but that it had nothing to do with Eric, that it was his grandfather who invited me. I say that I know the grandfather because I was hoping he could help me with some information I need. I don't go into what that information was. It isn't important to what happened, and I have a feeling it will only annoy Carver if he thinks I'm digressing. If he wants to know more about anything, he'll ask. I go straight to the part where I'm helping Eric and Duane with the fridge. I tell it all exactly how it happened. I don't leave out a single thing, and every word is the truth, which makes me feel more confident because if Carver questions me about any of it, he'll get the same answer every time. I won't be one of those idiots who tells a lie and then gets tripped up on it. I've done a lot of stupid stuff in my life, but this isn't going to be one of those times. This time I do it straight up. When I finish, the room is silent.

Carver looks steadily at me.

"A guy with a spider tattoo on his face, huh?"

"A giant one. It practically covered his whole face."

"You'd recognize him again, I suppose."

"I'd recognize that tattoo." How could anyone forget a thing like that?

"You say there was another guy there?"

I nod.

"We're recording this, Rennie. Say yes or no."

"Yes."

"Can you describe him?"

I think hard. "No, I can't." I was aware of someone else there, but I couldn't take my eyes off that spider.

More silence. Another look at the file folder. A shuffle of the few papers in there.

"Your fingerprints are on the murder weapon, Rennie. You want to explain that to me?"

There's something in the way he says it, like he's accusing me, that makes my leg jump again.

"You don't think *I* shot him, do you?"

"Did you?"

"No!"

"So, what, the fingerprint guys are wrong when they say the prints are yours?" He shakes his head. "I don't think so, Rennie."

I could kick myself. I realize I forgot the part about Spider Face throwing the gun at me. I went straight from him taking off after shooting Duane to me trying to help Duane. And now when I explain that to Carver—"The guy threw the gun at me"—it sounds lame. But it's the truth.

One of Carver's eyebrows arches.

"The killer threw his gun at you? Is that what you're telling me?"

I nod. I remember that I'm being recorded. "Yes. He said *hey*, then he threw the gun at me and I caught it."

Carver sighs. I'm not sure what that means. Maybe he can't believe I'm stupid enough to think he'll swallow what I'm dishing out. Maybe he thinks I'm the dumbest shooter he's ever met. Maybe he's just tired.

"You didn't mention that to the officers at the scene," he says finally. "Or when I asked you to tell me what happened. Did you just make that up, Rennie?"

"No!" I have never wanted anyone to believe me as badly as I want Detective Carver to now. "I'm telling you the truth. He threw it and I caught it. Kind of like a reflex." I'm beginning to think that my reflexes are not my best friend.

Carver is silent. Right about the time I start to sweat, he says, "Michigan was the first state to abolish the death penalty. Did you know that, Rennie?"

"No, sir." But I sure am glad to hear it.

"In 1846," Carver says. "Decades ahead of some states. At least a century before most of them. But that doesn't mean we're not tough on crime. You murder someone here, you pay. You murder a cop, you pay for the rest of your life."

Maybe Carver is one of those trivia buffs, and maybe he likes showing off. But I doubt it. Not in this situation anyway. I know that when the Major has to do a big interrogation, he prepares. I know because he tells me. According to the Major, preparation is the key to the success of every endeavor he can think of, from a military campaign to catching a wrong-doer to passing a history exam. The Major is like a Boy Scout that way. I think most military personnel are. Which makes me think this isn't just trivia Carver is spouting. There's a definite point behind it.

"I'm not sure I follow you," I say.

"The victim known to you as Duane—"

Known to me? What's going on?

"—was a police officer."

My leg starts in again, keeping time to a rocking drum solo I can't hear.

"He was a cop? I don't get it."

Carver's eyes are hard on me. "You're telling me you didn't know?"

"How would I know? I told you. I just met the guy. I didn't even know his name until tonight."

"He was a police officer, Rennie."

141

There's no way. "Why would a cop hang around with Eric?"

"Are you trying to tell me you don't know that either?" There's a bite to Carver's voice now, like he's well aware that I'm stringing him along and he doesn't appreciate it one little bit. But it isn't an act, and I'm not stringing him along.

"I told you. I don't really know Eric. I barely talked to him."

"Except to agree to do him a favor." Like, yeah, pull the other leg, Rennie.

"Yeah. That's exactly right." Now I'm not only scared, but I'm also angry. I didn't do anything wrong. Not this time. "I don't really know him. I didn't know Duane at all. I didn't know he was a cop. And I have no idea why a cop would be interested in a loser like Eric."

Carver perks up at the word *loser*.

"You ever been in Detroit before, Rennie?"

"No."

"And you say you never met Eric McLennan before?"

"That's right."

"What do you know about him?"

"Nothing. Except he lives with his uncle and his grandfather, he's got a major attitude problem, and he hangs with guys who look just like him—like losers."

Carver purses his lips. He's inspecting me carefully. "A couple of college kids were killed last spring."

It's my turn to perk up, and Carver notices.

"You heard about that, huh?" There's a flicker of a grin on his lips, like he thinks he's got me now.

"I was in a diner. It's a few blocks from where Eric lives. The cook is a guy named Jacques, from Ivory Coast. I met him my first night here and had breakfast there the next day. There were some guys in there when I was there. They were having breakfast. They said something about two college students getting killed by some white-power guys. If you want to, you can check with Jacques. He'll tell you."

Carver lets out a sigh. "A guy named Jacques is going to tell me that someone else mentioned two black kids who got murdered. What good is that going to do you, Rennie?"

"You'll know I'm not lying. I haven't lied about a single thing."

"You're concerned about that, are you? You're worried I don't believe you?"

That is a question a person in my situation doesn't want to have to answer. If I say I'm worried, he's going to press on why I should worry if, as I've been telling him, I didn't do anything wrong. If I say I'm not worried, he's going to wonder why I'm so confident, why I'm going into such elaborate detail, how far ahead I worked out my story, how well I planned what happened in that alley.

"Look," I say. "I came to Detroit to find out some information about my grandfather. That's how I met Eric's grandfather. He's a nice old guy. Eric lives with him. I don't know anything about Eric. When he asked me to help him out, I figured it was the least I could do. I was having supper at his place. His sister made it. I didn't know Duane. I didn't know he was a cop. And I don't know anything about those two college kids except what I heard in Jacques's diner. I don't even know why you brought them up." I have a bad feeling about that though.

"Two black college kids were killed in what we call a racially motivated crime." That was what the men in the diner had said, that they were killed by a group called the Black Legion. "One was beaten to death. The other was beaten and then shot. From what we were able to find out, it was some white kids who did it. For reasons I am not going to get into with you, we've determined Eric McLennan to be a person of interest in the case. Are you following me?"

"You think *Eric* did it?" I barely know the guy, but I wouldn't put it past him. He's got an attitude that I recognize only too well.

"Eric and a couple of his associates."

"So, what, Duane was undercover, trying to make the case?"

Of course, he doesn't answer. I don't think I expected him to. But I knew I was right. Duane had probably worked hard at getting close to Eric.

"Eric's pals," I say. "Do any of them have a spider tattoo?"

Carver rolls his eyes. "A giant one? One on his face? No, Rennie. None of Eric's known associates has a giant tattoo spider on his face."

Something about the way he says it makes me sweat. Does he believe me about the tattoo or doesn't he? Does he believe me about anything—or doesn't he?

"What about Eric?" I say.

"What about him?"

"He said he was going to turn the truck around so we could load the fridge. But he didn't. Maybe he knew Duane was a cop. So maybe he met up with Spider Face. Maybe he was with him."

Carver shakes his head. "Eric was at a gas station three blocks away. We have witnesses who say he was paying for gas when gunshots were heard. He's got an airtight alibi."

"And his friends? You said you think he and his friends killed those college students. Where were they when Duane got shot?"

Again, I get no answer.

"I didn't do anything wrong," I say. "I did CPR on him. Look, I could have been killed too."

Carver looks me straight in the eye. "But you weren't."

Silence.

"Are you going to arrest me?"

"Let me recap the situation for you, Rennie. We've got a dead cop. We've got a murder weapon with your fingerprints on it. We've got you with the victim's blood all over you. We've got exactly one witness to the killing—you. And you're telling me some guy with a giant spider tattoo on his face did it. That's what we've got."

Everything he says is factually true. But somehow the facts aren't working in my favor.

"I don't know you, Rennie. I don't know that anything you're telling me is true. You get what I'm saying?"

I do.

He stands up and sweeps the file folder off the table. "You stay put," he says.

I do exactly that. I sit in that hard chair at that bolted-down table in that drab tiny room, my leg beating as fast as my heart, and I wait. I don't know what I'm waiting for. To be told I can go, I guess. Definitely not to be told I'm under arrest. Definitely not that. I wait and I wish I'd never got that message from Adam. For sure I wish I'd never answered it. I wish I'd never come to Detroit.

An hour passes. I'm hot and tired and hungry. No one has offered me anything to eat or drink, which makes me think that things aren't going my way. Finally, the door opens and Carver comes back into the room. He has the file folder with him again, but it's thicker now. I get a very bad feeling. I sincerely hope he isn't about to read me my rights.

He sits down, leans back in his chair and looks me over.

"Rennie, you didn't tell me you have a record," he says. "Up there in Canada."

I tell him the truth, which is, "You didn't ask me."

He laughs. It's like a clap of thunder. I hear it and then it's gone, and you'd never know by looking around that it was ever there.

"Reads to me like you have a problem with impulse control, and maybe with keeping a lid on your temper."

"I guess that's true." Why not admit it? "I did have a problem with that."

"Did?"

"I'm working on it." Then, I suppose because I want him to see me in the best light possible, I add, "I'm back at school."

"Hmph." Which I read as, "So?"

"What do you think I should do, Rennie?" he says after a long pause. "What would you do if you were on my side of the table?"

I want to say, *Detective Carver, if I were you, I would kick me loose.* Because if he did that, I'd take myself to the nearest bus station, buy a ticket for

Windsor and zip across the border into good old Canada, and never look back. But trust me, the Major didn't raise anyone that stupid. It's not a real question. Carver isn't asking me to make a decision for him. He's playing with me. He's the big old cat, and I'm the little mouse he's flattened under his paw.

"Some people, my lieutenant, for example—" He nods at the mirror, which is only a mirror on this side of the wall. "He thinks I should arrest you and lock you up. He thinks we have everything we need to make this case: the murder weapon, the shooter, the motive."

"I had no reason to kill Duane," I tell him.

"So you say. But, see, that's part of the problem, Rennie. *You* say some guy with a spider tattoo shot Duane. *You* say you tried to save Duane's life. *You* say the murder weapon has your prints on it because the shooter threw the gun to you." He shakes his head again. "And then *you* say you had no reason to kill Duane."

I have to admit, if I were him I'd be a whole lot more than doubtful.

"So here's what I want you to do, Rennie."

I swallow hard. This is serious. Too serious.

"I want you to take a deep breath and tell me everything you've done from the minute you arrived in Detroit. I don't want you to leave anything out. Not a thing. You got that?"

I do. I start to talk.

TEN

My mind is racing. I go through the whole story from start to finish. I start with Adam. I hesitate before I say what Adam and the rest of my cousins found and what they're up to. It sounds even crazier than being shot at by a guy with a giant spider tattoo on his face. But by now it's obvious to me that this big homicide cop is the only thing standing between me and a jail cell. If I can convince him that every word I'm saying is true, I might have a chance to get out of here and go home.

I explain all about David McLean. Carver doesn't interrupt me. He doesn't get impatient and tell me to get to the point, that he doesn't want to hear anything about anyone's grandfather unless it's Eric's. The whole time I'm talking, he sits straight up in his chair, leaning forward slightly to make me think that he's catching every word I say, and I don't doubt he is.

I tell him about Buenos Aires and Mirella and Heinrich Franken. I tell him about Curtis and how he crossed paths with Mirella way back when. I say I was hoping that Curtis could help me out with more information. I tell him that's the only reason I'm in Detroit, that my being here has nothing to do with Eric McLennan. I tell him I don't even like the guy. I tell him everything. I don't leave anything out. At least, I don't think I do. My main goal: to convince Detective Carver that, despite what he knows from my record and from the circumstances in which he met me, I am basically a law-abiding citizen.

When I finish, Carver says nothing. Minutes tick by.

"That's it?" he asks finally. "That's everything?"

"That's everything."

I say it not because it's true. It's not. Not exactly. There's one little thing I don't tell him. It's not that I want to lie. What I want is for him to believe me. And it worries me that if I tell him this one thing, it'll make him take another hard look at me and decide to charge me and lock me up. I don't tell him about seeing Duane in Eric's garage, and I pray in my own way that it won't come back to bite me in the butt.

Carver gets up and leaves the room again. He's gone for a long time, during which I put my head down on the table and try to catch a little sleep. It's crazy, I know. One minute I'm so jumpy I'm like a perpetual-motion machine. The next, I'm exhausted.

Carver shakes me, hard.

I sit up. My neck is stiff. My mouth is dry. My stomach is rumbling.

Carver slides a can of pop in front of me. I snap it open and gulp greedily. He has a cup of coffee for himself. He sits down, again with the file folder.

"I've gotta tell you, Rennie," he says. "I've had a lot of people sit in that chair over the years, and a lot of them—most of them—have started by telling me cockamamie stories about how I've got the wrong person, how it couldn't possibly be them. If I was inclined, and I'm not, not even remotely, I could write a book. Seriously. You wouldn't believe the nonsense I've heard. Frankly, some of it is downright insulting. I didn't get here by being the dumbest cop on the beat."

That bad feeling I've had ever since I was put in this room gets dramatically worse.

"Your story, son…" He shakes his head. "It's the cockamamiest one I've ever heard, I kid you not. A grandfather with secret identities and a bunch of passports. Hidden money. Coded notes. It wouldn't even make a good novel. It's too crazy."

"But—"

His hand slashes through the air and makes me bite my tongue.

"Nobody would believe it," he says. "No cop I know. No sane jury member. Even a rookie defense attorney would advise you to come up with something better."

The soda in my belly starts churning like an ocean in the middle of a hurricane.

"If it wasn't for that thing you pulled off in Iceland," he says. He flips open the file folder, and there are some pages printed out from the Internet. About me. In Iceland. About what happened there. "And these guys—they're your cousins, right?" He flips the pages. There's a small article about my cousin Bunny, who got himself into a scrape with some gang members. *Thank you, Bunny*. There's a news item about Webb too, from some little newspaper way up north. "That whole idea, some guy leaving a video and sending his grandsons on these crazy missions—that's cockamamie too. But it looks to me like it's not the stories that are nuts. It was your grandfather. No offense."

"None taken," I say.

He leans back in his chair and studies me. "So you're here trying to track down what your grandfather had to do with some Nazi, huh?"

"I have a picture in my wallet." I start to reach for it and then stop. He nods. I pull my wallet out of my pocket and show him the copy of the newspaper photo Adam sent me. He looks at it and nods.

"Cockamamie," he says. "The thing is, Rennie, you have a record. You've been associating with a person of extreme interest in an unsolved murder instigated, we believe, by racial hatred. You were at the scene of the murder of a police officer. You're the only witness, and there are elements of the situation that put you in a very bad light. You understand that, right?"

"Yes, sir."

"And I'm sure you can understand that all of this makes my lieutenant antsy. Very antsy. He thinks that if I let you walk out of here, that even if I tell you not to leave town, that kind of thing, you'll shoot back across the border and give us a gigantic paperwork headache when we need you back down here again when and if this case goes to trial."

I hold my breath. Does that mean he believes my story? Or is this some kind of trick? Is he watching for my reaction? What's the best way for someone in my position to act? How do I make him believe I'm innocent?

"Now, I guess I could contact your father in Pakistan."

"Afghanistan," I say. "Sir."

"Afghanistan. I could tell him your situation and ask that he come back here."

"I wish you wouldn't do that." I wish it fervently.

"I bet you do." He sips his coffee. "My father was a military man too. A real disciplinarian."

"That's the Major," I say.

"Is there someone else you can contact? Another family member?"

"What for?"

"To come down here and talk to us. So maybe we can work something out."

My heart flutters. Is he going to let me go? If he does, is it because he believes me?

"There's my grandmother. She lives in Toronto."

He takes a notebook from his jacket pocket and slides it across the table together with a pen. "Write down her name and phone number."

I stare at the pen. I don't reach for it.

"I'd rather contact her myself. She'll freak out if a cop calls her." Especially a Detroit homicide cop. "She has no idea I'm even down here."

Carver sits still for a moment. "Okay," he says. "I'll get you a phone. You talk to her, and then I talk to her."

"I have my cell phone," I say.

There's a long pause.

"Okay. You call her. You talk to her. When you're done, you let me know and I'll talk to her." He stands up to leave. I can't shake the idea that he's setting a trap for me. But I say okay, and I pull out my cell phone and punch in my grandmother's phone number.

"Hello?"

The voice that answers isn't the one I'm expecting. It's not my grandmother. It's Ari. I think about hitting the End button—that's how much I like the guy.

But if I want to get out of this police station, I need to talk to my grandmother.

"Hey, Ari. Is my grandma around?"

"Rennie? I thought I recognized your number. Mel's been expecting you." That's my grandmother, Melanie. "To be honest, she's been worried. Is everything okay?"

See, that's the thing with Ari. You ask him a simple question—"Is my grandma there?"—but you don't get a simple, "Yes, I'll put her on." No, you get Ari's take on things. You get him asking you questions, like I even care what he thinks. And I don't. I don't care if he and Grandma have been best buddies since before I was born. I don't care if they visit back and forth—even though Grandma tells me there's absolutely nothing romantic going on between them. All I know is that Ari gives me the creeps. He asks too many questions. He watches people the way a fox watches a henhouse. And he's a know-it-all.

"I just need to talk to Grandma, Ari." I can't make it any plainer than that.

"She can't come to the phone right now."

"Why not? She's okay, isn't she?" Then I have a thought. I pray—boy, do I pray—that he's not going to tell me she's in the shower. I mean, it's bad enough that he's there at her place in the middle of the night. I glance at my watch. Correction: at six in the morning. But if I have to put it all together—Ari, early morning, Grandma in shower—I think I'll puke.

"She was at her friend Joyce's last night." Joyce and Grandma apparently raised hell back in the day. "They had a little too much wine, I think. She's sound asleep. And it *is* early. Can you call back later? Or do you want her to give you a shout?"

Before I can answer, I hear a sleepy voice. "Hello?"

"Grandma?"

"Rennie? Is that you?" She sounds instantly alert. "Where are you? Are you okay?"

"Sorry to wake you, Grandma."

"I've been worried. You were supposed to be here by now."

"I know. Something came up."

"You should have called. I was about to see if I could contact your father."

"No! Don't do that!"

I can't see my grandmother, and she doesn't say a word, but I have no trouble picturing her sitting straight up in bed now, her granny antennae quivering.

"What's going on, Rennie? You aren't in any trouble, are you? Maybe you'd better let me speak to Mr. Mitron."

"He's not here, Grandma. I mean, I'm not there. I'm not in Uruguay. I'm in Detroit."

"Detroit? What on earth are you doing there?"

"It's complicated."

"Uncomplicate it, Rennie." She sounds flinty now. She's nearly seventy, retired but far from inactive, and no one's idea of a grandmother. At least, she isn't my idea of one. She's fit and dresses like a million dollars, and no one pushes her around. She's one of the few people I know who can hold her own with the Major.

I glance at the mirror and wonder if Carver is behind it. Or if anyone else is. I know why I've been allowed to make this call, but I can't help asking something else before I get to the point.

"Grandma, did David McLean ever say anything to you about Argentina?"

"Argentina? I thought you said you were in Uruguay—before Detroit, I mean."

"I was. But I need to know about Argentina."

"I don't think I can help you, Rennie. I want you to come home. Now."

"I can't."

"Why not?"

"Like I said, it's complicated. Did he ever seem strange to you, Grandma? Or act strange? Or disappear sometimes?"

"Who?"

"David McLean."

"I don't like these questions, Rennie. Tell me where you are. I'll arrange a flight home for you and call you with the information."

Okay, there's no avoiding it now.

"The thing is, Grandma, I'm at a police station."

"Police station?" She does not like the sound of that.

"It's okay." At least, I sincerely hope it is. "There was a mix-up."

"What kind of a mix-up?"

"Someone got killed."

"Killed?"

I hear Ari in the background, asking what this is all about and who got killed.

"Rennie, are you okay?"

"I'm fine, Grandma. There's just been a mix-up, that's all." I'm on my feet and walking to the door of the interrogation room. I can't wait to hand the phone to Carver. "There's a detective here who wants to talk to you, Grandma."

"Detective? What detective?"

"His name is Carver. He's a homicide detective."

Carver is waiting in the hall, still working on his coffee. When he hears his name, he comes away from the filing cabinet he was leaning against and starts for me. I hand him the phone.

"It's my grandmother."

"Name?"

"Melanie Cole."

Carver takes the phone. "Mrs. Cole? Detective Dan Carver, Detroit Police."

Then Carver is talking to her. His voice is calm. He tells her that I've witnessed something and that because I'm a foreign national and a minor, he'd appreciate if she could come down here and do some paperwork, because they might need me to return sometime in the future as the case progresses and he wants to make sure that's not going to be a problem. He spends a lot of time with her, and he stays calm and seems to answer most of her questions—although, of course, some of the answers are,

"I'm afraid I can't go into that, ma'am. It's an ongoing investigation." But he does assure her that I'm okay.

I guess they work things out, because he turns to me and says, "She plays hardball, your grandma." He doesn't explain. He just hands the phone back to me, and the next thing I know, my grandma is giving me a lecture on getting my butt back to my hotel room and staying there until she gets there. "Don't you even think about not being there when I arrive, Rennie, because I will call your father if I have to." Translation: She's angry and—if you want my opinion—a little scared, and she will not hesitate to bring in the big guns (the Major) if I give her even an iota of trouble.

I tell her no problem. I tell her I don't want trouble any more than she does. That part is true. Trouble is the last thing I want. The part about staying put— well, I came here for a reason, and there's no way I'm going to let Eric stop me from making a last attempt to get what I want.

Carver makes me hand over my passport and my driver's license.

"So you don't get the urge to leave me flat," he says. "And so you'll plant yourself in your hotel room and stay there until your granny gets there."

I sign a receipt for my ID. I sign some other papers. Carver gives me his card, and I agree to check in with him. I give him my cell number so that he can check in with me. I listen to his lecture about doing what my grandma said. Then he lets me walk free.

ELEVEN

By now I've been wearing the same clothes for days. When I leave the police station, I think about heading over to Jacques's diner to pick up my duffel bag. But then I pass a discount store. It's right there, a couple of blocks from where I'm staying. So I deke inside and pick up new underwear, socks and a T-shirt. I also buy a pair of gloves. I'm tired of my hands freezing all the time. I start back to the hotel, dreaming the whole way about a long hot shower followed by something to eat.

I see the Holiday Inn. I turn to go in the front door. Someone says, "Spare some change?"

I look down. There's a guy about my age sitting cross-legged on the sidewalk. He's bareheaded. He has a cap—a baseball-type cap, not a warm hat—but it's on the cement in front of him instead of on his head. There's a handful of coins in it. He looks up at me.

"Spare some change for a hot meal?" he says.

I look him over. Usually I'm not in much of a position to hand out cash. But it's freezing cold, it's New Year's Eve, there aren't many people on the street, and this guy looks like he could use something to eat even more than I could. But before I can dip into my pocket, a guy in a suit with a hotel name tag pinned to it—a Thomas Hadley clone—rushes out the door and tells us both to get lost.

"I'm sick of you people hanging around out here bothering our guests," he says. "I've called security. They're on their way to clear you off."

The guy on the sidewalk laughs at that. "Right," he says. "Like a panhandler is going to make the top of their list."

The suit glowers at him. He turns and snaps his fingers, and two burly guys in security-guard uniforms come at us. One grabs me. The other hauls the panhandler to his feet.

"Get out of here now," the suit says. "Get a job."

The panhandler draws himself up straight. "I have a job." He looks at the guard whose hand is clamped like a vise around my arm. "You know it, too. You bought a car at Honest John's. You've seen me there."

The guard's face changes slowly from growling animal to surprised recognition. "Yeah, right. You're the kid who sweeps up. You wash cars, too, when it's warmer."

The panhandler nods. "Yeah. And I do security at night sometimes, so we're practically colleagues."

The suit snorts, like, *right!* "If you had a job, you wouldn't be harassing my guests," he says.

"It's not my fault the job doesn't pay enough," the kid says. "A guy's got to make ends meet."

"Well, make them meet somewhere else," the suit says. To the guards, he says, "Get them out of here."

The two burly guards start to manhandle us down the street.

"Hey! I'm staying here," I say.

Nobody listens to me. The two guards muscle us until we're all the way down the block. Then they march back into the lobby.

I look at the panhandler. I pull out my wallet and hand him a couple of twenties. Then I pull the tuque off my head and give that to him too.

"Keep your head warm, and it'll keep the rest of you warmer," I tell him.

He puts on the tuque and pulls it down over his forehead, smiling.

"Thanks."

"No problem."

I march back to the hotel, push my way into the lobby and am halfway to the elevators when the suit shows up again.

"I thought I told you—"

I flash him my room card. He insists I follow him to the front desk, where he checks the room number in the computer. He demands to see identification. I fight the urge to deck him and reach for my passport. But I don't have it. Detective Carver does. I show him my credit card again. He snorts.

"How do I know it's not stolen?"

"Thomas Hadley checked me in. He saw my ID."

The guard shakes his head. His eyes dart somewhere over my shoulder.

"Mr. Hadley!"

I turn and there he is.

"This…*person* says you know him," the suit says.

Hadley looks me over. "He's a guest."

"He doesn't have ID."

"I said he's a guest, Lionel."

Lionel must be an underling, because he backs down. I'm free to make my way to the elevators. I pass Thomas Hadley on the way.

"Just out of curiosity," he says, "what happened to your ID?"

"You sure you want to know?"

He considers the question. "Have a pleasant stay." He continues on through the lobby.

I go up to my room, where I strip, shower and change into the clean things I just bought. I think about breakfast. I look at the bed.

When I wake up, it's late afternoon. There's a message on my phone. It's my grandmother, telling me that she'll arrive sometime tonight and warning me, again, to stay put. It sounds like the sensible thing to do, but I have unfinished business. Besides, what she doesn't know won't hurt me.

I walk from the hotel to the old man's place. It's colder out than it was earlier in the day, and now I don't have a hat. Stupid-looking as it was, it kept my head warm. And what I told the panhandler is true—when your head is warm, so is the rest of you. I stop along the way to buy another tuque. The selection at the place where I stop is as bad as it was at the airport. Don't you know it, I end up with another red-and-white-striped hat, this one even goofier than the last one.

But it's warm, and it's not like I'm trying to impress anyone.

When I get to the house, Eric is outside, tossing handfuls of salt onto the front walk.

"Hey," he says when he sees me. "You okay? Last time I saw you, you were shaking like a wet dog."

"Where were you?" I ask. "Didn't they question you?"

"The cops? Yeah. But I was gassing up. I missed all the action. What happened?"

I look at him, this time with a bunch of questions bumping up against each other in my head. For example: This murder the cops are looking at him for—is that why Katya is so determined to get him out of town? Is that what she wants him to put behind him? If it is, then it sounds like she thinks the cops have it all wrong, like she doesn't believe her little brother Ricky could hurt anyone, let alone beat them and shoot them.

For example: Despite what Katya might think, did Eric do it? Is Carver right, and am I looking at the guy who not only decided to kill two black college kids, but who actually went through with it? Carver says he's pretty sure there were a couple of guys with him. He didn't say what role he thought they played. What he said was that Eric was a person of interest. Just Eric. He didn't mention anyone else by name.

For example: Does Eric know that Duane was a cop? Does that have anything to do with what happened last night? Or was last night's shooting just some crazy, random thing that happens in a run-down city where no one has a decent job and anyone who can afford to leave has already hightailed it out of town?

"What do you mean, what happened?" I say.

"I mean, how did it go?"

"I'm standing here, aren't I?"

He looks at me through slit-narrow eyes and nods. "Were you able to help them out?"

I give him one of the Major's patented looks, like I don't know what he means and if he wants an answer, he's going to have to explain.

"You never told me what happened in that alley," he says.

It's true. The whole time we were waiting for the ambulance back there at the mouth of that alley, I didn't open my mouth. I think—I can't remember exactly—that Eric might have said something. Maybe he asked me a question. Maybe he asked me a hundred of them. But I didn't answer. I kept seeing Spider Face and the gun in his hand. Then Duane, not moving. I kept remembering how I squatted down and my hand that touched the ground came away all sticky, and I couldn't see what it was, even though I knew it was blood. I didn't see it clearly until I came out of that alley, until the paramedics had me in the back of their truck and were checking me out. That's when I got a clear look at my hands and at the whole front of myself. That's when I saw all that blood.

"There's not much to tell," I say. "We went back to get that fridge, like you said. Some guys showed up. One of them shot Duane." I start shaking again just remembering it. "If you'd pulled the truck around like you said you would, if you'd shone some light back there, maybe it wouldn't have happened."

"What?" He's staring at me like I just grew a second head. "You're blaming *me* for Duane getting shot?"

"It was your fridge. We were doing you a favor. Why didn't you do what you said you were going to do?"

"I told you. I was getting gas. You didn't want to have to carry that fridge back here on your back, did you?"

Like I would have done that!

"Look," he says, lowering his voice. "Look, I'm sorry about what happened. Duane was a good guy, and I hope the cops get whoever did this. That's why I asked you if you were able to help them out."

Eric is about the same height as me, but stockier. He's got no hair under that cap on his head, but if he had, it would probably be black like his eyebrows, which are thick and almost meet over the bridge of his nose. His eyes are as dark as his eyebrows, and they're filled with emotion now. The thing is, I can't tell whether the emotion I'm seeing is the real deal or if he's faking it.

He leans in to me. "What did you tell them?"

"What do you think? I told them exactly what happened."

"The guys who did it, did you see them?"

"I saw the main guy."

"So you described him to the cops?" He's all eager, like, good for me, maybe I've given them what they need to crack this case.

"The guy had a massive tattoo on his face."

"A tattoo?"

"A spider. It covered practically his whole face. There can't be that many guys around who look like that."

"What else?"

"What do you mean?"

"Did you recognize him?"

"No!" Why would I? I don't know anyone in town. Besides, all I remember—all I could tell Carver—was that tattoo. There wasn't time for anything else.

"This guy. Did he see you, Rennie?"

"I guess so. I mean, he must have seen me as well as I saw him."

Eric's expression is somber. "Then you'd better be careful."

"Me? What for?"

"You saw a guy shoot and kill someone right in front of you. That's what happened, right?"

"Yeah."

"And he saw you. Geez, think about it, Rennie. You're an eyewitness to a murder."

"Right." A pretty useless eyewitness, if you ask me. I glance up at the house. "I'm going home tonight," I tell him. "Back to Canada until the cops here need me. I just wanted to say goodbye to your grandfather. Is he home?"

"Yeah. He's in his room. Go on in, if you want. The door's open."

The door to the house is open. The door to the old man's room isn't. When I knock, he wants to know who it is. When I say it's me, there's only silence. When I knock again, he says, "Keep your shirt on!" It's another minute before he unlocks the door, opens it a couple of inches and squints out at me.

"What do you want?"

He sounds angry. Looks angry too. At first, I think he doesn't remember me.

"You're here to quiz me about Nazis, aren't you?" he demands.

"You said you were going to see if you could find out anything about a guy named Franken," I remind him. "The man I think Mirella was married to."

"And you said you would tell me why you wanted to know. But you didn't. You haven't told me a damn thing."

I don't know for sure what flew up his nose, but he's angry, all right. Good and angry. He's standing in the sliver of space between the door and the frame, blocking it with his walker and scowling at me like I'm an Amway salesman.

"If you don't want to talk to me, just say so," I say. "I'll leave." Actually, I have no intention of leaving until I find out if he knows anything. But I'm hoping he'll calm down.

His sour expression stays firmly in place, but he backs up his walker a pace and throws open the door so I can come in. But he doesn't sit down and doesn't invite me to take a seat either. He says, "Why are you so interested in this fellow Franken?"

I already told Detective Carver what I was doing here, so the secret's out. I can't do any more harm by telling Curtis. I pull out my wallet and take out the two pictures from Adam. I hand him the one from the newspaper.

"My cousin sent me this," I say.

Curtis squints at the picture. He makes his way to a cluttered table, sits down and switches on a lamp so he can take a better look. Then he says, "Glasses. Table beside the bed." I go over to the bedside table but don't see any glasses. "Drawer," he says. I open the drawer and find a massive glasses case. It holds one of those giant pairs of glasses that old men seem to like—don't ask me why. They cover more face than eye. He slips them on and takes another look. I can't tell if he recognizes the face or not.

"It's the one that's circled," I say.

"I get that," he grumps at me. "That's an SS uniform. This man was in the SS." He puts the picture down. "And this is supposed to be Franken?"

"As far as I can tell. I know he lived in Buenos Aires for a while after the war. I talked to a woman who was a little girl when he moved there. And when he left."

"Franken." Curtis looks out into space. "This woman. What did she say about him?"

"Just that he lived there and that he married a woman named Mirella."

He leans back in his chair. "Mirella Gutierrez."

"I guess. She didn't say." And I could kick myself for not asking.

"What does your cousin have to do with this?"

"My cousin isn't involved. But he sent me this picture too. It's—"

Curtis goes still when I give him the second picture. It's like he's stopped breathing or something.

"Are you okay?" I ask. He's staring at the picture, his eyes wide behind his enormous glasses. "Do you recognize him?"

He looks at me and then back at the picture.

"What do you know about this man?" he asks. His voice is hoarse.

"I'm trying to figure stuff out," I say. "You've seen him before, haven't you?"

Curtis spits on the photo—a big, juicy hork. He starts to get up from his chair but doesn't make it. He crumples. I grab him, afraid that whatever happened a couple of nights ago is happening again now. But he rallies.

"He's a spy," he says. "He tried to recruit my father. He's responsible for what happened to him."

"What did happen?"

"He died. My father died."

TWELVE

I'm so stunned by what Curtis tells me that I almost fall over.

Is it true? Was David McLean really a spy? I wonder how Curtis's father died and what role David McLean played.

"Are you sure?" I ask. But the facts all seem to fit. David McLean went down to South America with an Argentinian passport. He was using a German name. He offered Franken a job in the States. And I know next to nothing about David McLean except that he had a relationship with my grandmother, which explains me, and he had a secret, which explains why I'm here. "How do you know?"

The old man's eyes are drilling into me. "I know. Believe me, I know. He was a ruthless man working for a ruthless government, one with no conscience."

What was he talking about? What government? The Russians? The Chinese? They were supposedly the enemy back in the sixties.

"What do you mean, ruthless?"

"Just what I said. He came to my father. He recruited him. He was responsible for what happened next."

"To your father?"

Curtis nods.

"What do you mean?" I ask. "What happened exactly?"

"He died in a Russian labor camp." Curtis shoves the picture back at me, but it's covered in his spit and I don't want to touch it. He lets it fall to the floor. "How did your cousin get that picture? What do you want?"

I consider my answer carefully. I feel that I owe Curtis something. He's helped me do what I came here for.

"The man in that picture is my grandfather," I say.

Curtis stares at me. "Your grandfather?"

"My cousins found that picture and some other stuff. I—we just wanted to know what they were all about."

"Well, now you do. So I'll thank you to leave. Immediately. And never come back."

"But my grandfather—he was a good man. A nice man."

"Really?" Like he didn't believe me. "How well did you know him? How well does one generation ever know another? How well do you really know your own father? He's a soldier, isn't that right? Do you have any idea of the things he's done? Do you? Does he ever talk about his experiences to you? Go back another generation, to your grandparents, and what do you know? Really know, I mean?"

"I know he was my grandfather. I—"

"Answer me this. What were his parents' names?"

"What? What does that have to do with anything?"

"Do you know or don't you?"

I don't. I shake my head.

"There you go," the old man says. "You don't even know their names. It doesn't take long to forget, does it?" His stare is withering. "That man"—he means

David McLean—"acted like a friend to my father. I have pictures of them together, looking like they'd known each other forever. I took them myself. My father gave me a camera—I remember it. I took pictures, and I still have them."

I want to see them. I want to see the American whose death my grandfather is responsible for. I also want to know exactly what happened.

"Can I see them?" I ask.

"No, you cannot."

"Can you at least tell me what happened?"

"Leave. Now."

"But I didn't do anything. Whatever my grandfather did, it's not my fault."

The old man is swaying in his chair. When I ask him if he's okay, he barks at me that he's just fine, thank you very much. But I don't believe him. It's hot in here. I'm hot.

"I'll get you some more water." There's a jug on the far side of the bed. I pick up a glass and fill it. I try to open the window, too, to get a little air in. But it's locked. I swivel the locking mechanism and start to open it again.

"Leave it," the old man says. "Do you want to kill me with the cold? It's bad enough I have to go out on a night like this."

I remember that Katya and Noah are taking the family to dinner. I look at the window, leave it as it is and carry the glass of water back to the old man. He takes it but doesn't say a word.

"I'm sorry," I tell him. "I don't know exactly what happened. I don't know what David McLean did to your father. But I'm sorry."

He won't look at me. In a way, I can't blame him. There's nothing else I can do. I leave.

I leave, but I plan to go back. I have to. Somewhere in the old man's room are pictures of my grandfather. What will they tell me? Is there proof somewhere in them of the double life he led? I came all this way. I need to know. I need to see them.

Part of me says it doesn't matter. Whatever happened, it was a long, *long* time ago. David McLean is dead. Maybe—probably—I'll never know why he hid all his spy stuff instead of burning it. As for what kinds of things he did while he was a spy, well, it doesn't matter what the crime is; the statute of limitations runs out when the suspect dies. You can't get blood from a stone—or from the dead. End of story.

But the truth is, for some reason I can't figure out, it matters to me. This man was my grandfather. He was my mom's dad. I met him, and he seemed like a good guy. I felt that he understood me. I felt he cared. And now someone is telling me he was anything but good, that basically he was a traitor who did terrible things to people, like condemn them to Russian labor camps. What kind of a person would do such a thing? And why? What was he thinking?

Maybe I'll never know the answer to that— assuming it's true. Maybe the best I can do is figure out if what the old man told me is accurate, or if he's just a confused old coot who doesn't know what he's talking about. After all, how long has it been since he supposedly saw David McLean? And what if the man in his so-called proof pictures only resembles my grandfather but isn't really him? I owe it to myself to find out. In a weird way, I feel I owe it to my grandfather too.

I walk past closed-down stores. I'm not sure where I'm going. I check my watch. The whole family is going out to some fancy restaurant to celebrate Noah and Katya's engagement. As soon as the house is empty, I'm going back in. In the meantime, I have time to kill.

I take a left and head up a residential street—well, what used to be a residential street—aiming for the lights in the distance, for downtown. Maybe I can hang out someplace warm. Maybe in a store. Or a coffee shop.

There's a parking lot up ahead. Correction: it's a used-car lot. When I get closer, I can see the neon sign–*Honest John's*—but the neon is switched off. Maybe Honest doesn't see any advantage in paying for electricity on a night when no one is likely to buy a car. Or maybe he's having trouble paying his bills. His lot is crammed with cars. Too many, if you ask me. Honest has obviously been buying, but it looks like he's had a little trouble selling. In the distance, on the other side of the lot, I see the sign for a coffee place. I can hang out there for a while. I cut across the used-car lot.

I'm about a third of the way in when something zings past me, and the driver's-side window of the car next to me shatters. What the—?

Another zing. Something slams into the car in front of me. I can't see what it is, but I have a bad feeling.

I hear footsteps somewhere behind me. Someone is running. Maybe two someones. Maybe more. I have no idea. All I know is, the footsteps are getting louder, which means they're heading toward me.

I hear another sound, louder this time. Another car window explodes. Someone is shooting. At me.

Every muscle in my body freezes up, and I remember what Eric said. I saw the guy who shot Duane, and the shooter saw me. I told Carver I could recognize him. Who couldn't, with a tattoo like that? But at the same time, I told myself I was safe because the shooter has no idea who I am. He's never seen me before. I'm not from here.

Now I think: He doesn't need to know who I am. Maybe it's enough that he knows who I was with, and I was with Duane. The shooter must have known Duane. He shot him dead, just like that. So maybe he also knew who Duane hung out with. Maybe he knew that Duane was buddies with Eric. He'd probably assume I was too. That would have given him some kind of clue about where to find me. I've just come from Eric's house. Another thought—the guys at Jacques's diner said everyone knows who killed those college kids. Maybe someone was impatient with the cops. Maybe someone had decided to take the law into his own hands.

Yet another thought: What if the shooter knew Duane was a cop? What if he had a grudge against Duane because of that? And there I was, watching him take down a cop. I can ID him. I can say, "That's the guy who shot that cop." If I was the shooter, I'd want to get rid of me the fastest and easiest way possible. The smart thing would be to have someone watch me when I came out of the police station. Maybe that same person had followed me back to my hotel. And then to Eric's place. And then…

I keep my head down. I keep my whole body down. And I run, but not in a straight line. That would be stupid. I zigzag between the cars. I pray that someone else hears the shots and calls the cops. I try not to think about the thirty minutes it supposedly takes to get a 9-1-1 response in this town, assuming there's a citizen around who's concerned enough to make the call.

I fumble in my pocket for my cell phone. Why wait for a stranger to do something when you can do it yourself?

Someone rears up in front of me, a guy in a bala-clava. He has a gun, and it's pointed at me. I start to raise my hands in a gesture of surrender. What else can I do? Through the balaclava's mouth hole, I see the guy grin. He turns his head a little, probably to call to his buddies: *Hey, I got him, he's here.* But he doesn't get out a single word, because in that split second I dive forward, tackling him at the knees, taking him down. The gun goes off. The guy is flat on his back, cursing. I don't stick around for his buddies to show up. I roll under the closest car and then under the one beside it. I keep going, dragging myself from car to car, all the weight on my elbows. All I can think is, Keep moving.

I hear more footsteps. I see boots, or think I do. It's as dark as the bottom of a pit under those cars. I dig for my phone again, but my pocket is empty. I must have dropped it, or it fell out of my pocket. I see feet moving slowly. They're looking for me. If I stay where I am, I'm dead.

If I move, I'm probably dead too.

Still, I drag myself under another car, and then another. Honest John's place is huge, and I have no idea how many more cars I'll have to crawl under before I get to the edge of the lot. I also don't know if there's someone patrolling the perimeter, waiting for me.

I can't hear anything. I can't tell if they're still there or if they've given up.

Suddenly, someone is running.

I hear someone shout, "Got him!"

I hear shots—three of them.

But I'm still in one piece.

I see feet again. They're two cars away from where I'm hiding. I see someone crouch down. Then: "Hey! Hey, what's going on out there?"

I hear a blast.

"I'm sick to death of you guys ripping me off!"

Another blast.

Something shatters—I'm thinking more car windows. The same voice lets out a stream of curses. They sound like poetry the way they're strung together.

Something clatters to the frozen ground.

I hear more running, and suddenly the lot is flooded with light.

I stay put.

I see feet again—and the end of what looks like a shotgun barrel. I hear another curse, soft and sad. I hear footsteps running. When I roll out from under the car, I see a man racing into the car dealership's office. Honest John, maybe, standing guard? I don't stick around to find out. I stay on my hands and knees where (I hope) he can't see me. As soon as the man with the shotgun is inside, with his back to me—I think he's on the phone—I crouch-run through the maze of cars. I see something glinting on the ground— my phone. I grab it.

A few paces farther and I stumble and fall to my knees. What I've stumbled over: a guy lying on the pavement, half under a car. He's young like me, but scruffy and rough-looking, and he's wearing my hat. I feel a jolt when I realize he's the panhandler from outside my hotel, the guy the shift manager wanted to shift right off his turf, telling him to get a job and leave the guests alone. The guy I gave a couple of twenties and my hat to. He said he had a job. He said that he worked part-time security at a car lot but it didn't pay the bills. Looks to me like he wasn't too good at his job.

I feel bad about what happened to him. I really do. It makes me want to go home more than ever.

But mostly, given what happened the last time someone got shot and killed in my vicinity, it makes me want to get away—now.

I keep low until I'm clear of Honest John's. Then I run as fast and as far as I can. I run until my lungs are ready to burst. Until they hurt every time I take a breath and feel like they're lined with ice, it's that cold out. I haven't seen a single police car or heard a single siren. If Honest John has managed to scare up any law enforcement, they're going in silent. And invisible.

THIRTEEN

I'm a good dozen blocks from Honest John's and shaking all over, like one of those nutcases who start the New Year by pulling on their swim trunks and jumping into a nearly frozen lake as if it were the middle of July. My head is spinning. I need to think. So I duck into a greasy spoon—one of the few places that's open on the mostly boarded-up block I'm on—and grab a booth at the back, as far away as possible from the windows. There's no waitress, just a bored-looking guy behind the counter who calls to me, "What'll it be, sport?"

"Coffee," I tell him. And there it is again. My stomach. It's growling. You'd think I'd be in shock or something. Maybe I am. Or maybe I'm getting used to all this shooting. But I'm also hungry. My grand-mother says lately it's like I have a hollow leg—she doesn't know where I put all the food I consume. "You do burgers?" I ask.

The guy at the counter rolls his eyes and raises one index finger to point to the display board that runs the length of the grill, the milkshake maker, the coffeemakers—the whole wall behind the counter. There are pictures of every food item, in case the patrons can't read, I guess. Yeah, they do burgers.

"Cheeseburger," I say. "With fries." I look at the pictures. "And gravy. On the side."

The guy nods. He turns to the grill. I watch him bend. When he straightens up, he drops a patty onto the grill, and I hear it sizzle. He brings me a mug and a couple of creamers and pours coffee from what looks like a fresh pot. Could also be a full pot that's been sitting on the warmer for hours. There's no one else in the place except him and me. Maybe the supper rush hasn't started yet. Maybe there is no supper rush. He goes back to the grill, and I think about what just happened.

There's no doubt in my mind that those guys were gunning for me. I didn't see any faces this time, but there's also no doubt in my mind that they're the same guys who showed up in that alley and shot Duane and who probably would have shot me if Spider Face hadn't heard that sound up on the fire escape. They must have been watching the police station. They must have been looking for me so they could stop me from identifying them to the cops. Lucky for me that they got the wrong guy. Not so lucky for the panhandler that I gave him my hat.

I know what I should do: call Detective Carver.

The fry guy is back with my cheeseburger, fries and side of what turns out to be the best gravy I've ever tasted—better even than my grandmother's, and let me tell you, she is the queen of gravy. I dig in. My hands stop shaking. Something approaching calm settles over me like a big, comfy, grandma-knit sweater. I chase the food down with the rest of my coffee and, what do you know, the fry guy is back, pouring me a refill. It's definitely fresh. It's as good as the gravy. I wonder where all his customers are. The guy knows his way around a kitchen.

While I sip my refill, I think about what Carver is going to say when he hears from me. I imagine a supremely skeptical look on his face as he says,

"So, Rennie, you *say* some guys started shooting at you in a used-car lot, is that right? Did you get a good look at them? No? But you're sure they're the same guys who shot Duane? How do you know? You *say* they were wearing balaclavas and that's why you didn't get a good look at them tonight? That's funny, don't you think, considering that you didn't say anything about balaclavas last night when Duane was shot, especially when the one you saw clearly, the shooter, had such a distinguishing feature. It was a big spider tattoo on his face, isn't that what you said? Why do you think they would wear balaclavas tonight, when they go out to eliminate the eyewitness—that is what you're claiming, right, Rennie? That they came after you because you saw what they did last night? So why did they wear balaclavas tonight but they didn't wear them last night? I mean, according to your theory, you already saw them, so it's not like they have anything to hide. In fact, it would make a whole lot more sense if they'd worn balaclavas *last night*, to avoid being recognized in the first place."

Which is a darn good point.

Another thing I imagine Carver saying: "You claim that these guys came after you and that they tried to kill you, but instead the dead body we have is some semi-homeless guy who you say you *happened* to run into outside your hotel. You say you felt bad for him when the shift manager ran him off and you went after him and gave him a few bucks, and that's when you also gave him your hat. He told you he had a part-time job at a used-car lot—that's what you claim, right? Did he tell you it was Honest John's? He did, didn't he, Rennie?" I remember now that he did. He mentioned it to one of the security guards, who, if the police check, will confirm it. "And now he's dead. Not you, Rennie, but this guy you *happened* to run into and who probably seems like he's disposable. Is that what you think, Rennie? That because he's down and out, he's worthless, something you just use and throw away, like toilet paper?"

Can you tell I've lived my whole life with the armed forces version of the Grand Inquisitor? Or that I've had a run-in or two with the cops? I know how these guys think. They're so predictable, it's almost depressing. I can play out the whole thing in my head.

Carver: "I don't suppose there were any witnesses to what you *say* happened tonight, were there, Rennie? Oh, Honest John was there? Well, let me ask you this.

According to what you told me, he didn't show up with his shotgun until after a whole lot of gunplay. That *is* what you said, isn't it? So where was he before that? He surprised you, didn't he, Rennie? The place looked deserted. Hell, it was deserted except for you and your victim."

Me: "Wait a minute. *My* victim?"

I imagine my cockamamie story looking even more cockamamie now. I imagine Carver retracting the benefit of the doubt he extended to me now that there have been two shootings and I'm the only witness to both. It's the kind of thing that makes a good cop wonder.

Carver: "You were there, Rennie. But you didn't call it in. The only reason we know there's been a shooting is that we got the call from Honest John."

I'd stake my life on that being true.

Carver: "You didn't stick around this time either, did you, Rennie? Too bad, because your story might have been believable if you had. I don't know exactly what's going on here, Rennie, or where you fit in. But the balaclava thing? I don't know if you're brain-dead or what, but it was dumb to add that part. You know why? Because it doesn't make any sense."

And he would be right if he said that. It doesn't make any sense.

I get stuck on that while I drink my second cup of coffee. How come the shooters show their faces to me when they kill a cop, but they hide their faces in a deserted used-car lot when they try to take me out?

Could be that they didn't see me last night until it was too late, just like Spider Face probably would have finished me off and left me lying on the street alongside Duane if that door on the fire escape hadn't clanged when it did?

And then I get stuck on something else.

I think about what I almost told Carver back at the police station but didn't because I was afraid he'd think I had something to do with what happened to Duane. I wish now that I'd spoken up. Because if I tell him now, I can imagine how *that* conversation will go.

Me: "There's something I should have told you."

Carver: "Yeah? What's that?"

Me: "When I left Eric's house yesterday (was it really only yesterday?), after I talked to the old man, I saw this suspicious guy lurking around the garage. It turned out it was Duane. I didn't know who he was then. I'd never seen him before. He was at the side door to the garage, and he was acting strange, like he wanted to make sure no one saw him—you know what I mean?"

Carver says nothing.

Me: "He went inside."

Carver: "And?"

Me: "Like I said, he looked suspicious. So I decided to take a look. I found him in the garage. He had a flashlight, and he was looking around. I watched him for a few seconds before he spotted me. He saw something and was reaching for it."

Carver: "What was it?"

Me: "A box. It was up on this storage shelf."

Carver: "Did you see what was in it?"

Me: "No. I said, 'Hey.' He shoved the box back onto the shelf, grabbed a shovel and left the garage. When we got outside, Eric was there. He wanted to know what we were doing. Duane said he was going to clear the driveway. I left. But when I looked back, he was gone and Eric was going into the garage. The thing is, I told Eric that Duane was in the garage looking for something. I didn't say what it was, and he didn't ask. But I did tell him."

Carver: "That's some story, Rennie. How come you didn't tell me that before?"

I know what Carver would be thinking at this point. He'd be thinking I was the one who tipped off Eric to Duane being a cop. I was the one who was responsible for Duane getting killed. And now I was responsible for someone else getting killed, another innocent person. He was probably also going to wonder what else I hadn't told him. For sure he wouldn't let me walk out of the police station again.

But the main reason, the number-one reason, I don't call Carver right away is that I want to get back into the old man's room. I want whatever it is that proves David McLean was a spy. I want to know what he did to Curtis's father. I won't be able to do that if I call Carver because Carver will want to question me again. He'll want me to go over everything that happened—again. It will be a miracle if he believes me. And I will have blown the one and only chance I have to get to the truth about David McLean and put this whole secret-identity thing behind me forever.

The phone in my pocket vibrates.

It's probably my grandmother, checking in on me again.

I pull out the phone and see right away that not only is it not my grandmother, but it's not even my phone.

Somebody else must have dropped this phone in the used-car lot—maybe one of the shooters—and I picked it up, thinking it was mine.

It's not a call either. It's a text message: Did you get him?

That could mean anything. For example, it could mean, did the owner of the phone—one of the shooters—get me? Did he kill me?

I check out more of the messages stored in the phone. My whole body tenses up. I can't believe what I'm reading, but there it is, in digital black and white. Well, black on a green background for the old messages. Black on blue for the latest one.

I scroll through the phone's contact list. I slump in the booth. This phone, I realize, is golden. As long as I don't lose it, I don't have to worry about Carver. I can do what I have to do and after that I can settle this business.

As long as no one shoots at me again.

I check my watch. If Katya and Noah are taking the family out to dinner, for sure they're on their way by now. I pay for my food and walk back to Curtis's house for what I sincerely hope is the last time. On the way, I stop at what's turning out to be my favorite discount store to buy a flashlight and some batteries.

I get to the house in time to see Gerry helping his father down the porch steps. The old man has his walker, but he's struggling to get it over the uneven concrete of the walk. He curses. Gerry has to hold him with one hand and keep lifting the walker with the other. They inch their way to the truck parked in the driveway. Gerry finally gets the old man around to the passenger door and inside. He slams the door shut and bellows for Eric.

Eric appears. "I don't even want to go," he says.

"Tough. You're coming with us if I have to hogtie you and throw you in the back."

I guess Gerry is tough, because Eric doesn't argue anymore. He shuts the front door, locks it and slouches his way to the truck, where he climbs in beside the old man. Gerry gets behind the wheel and starts the engine. The truck splutters but finally does what it's supposed to. I watch the three of them back down the driveway in that rusted-out piece of junk and wonder if the place where Noah is planning to wine and dine them has valet parking. If it does, I'd love to see the face of the guy who gets handed the keys. He's not going to expect a big tip from Gerry, and he likely won't get one.

I wait until the taillights have disappeared around the corner before I slip to the back of the house.

I left the old man's window unlocked, and nobody has locked it again. Piece of cake, I think.

Wrong. I find out pretty fast that the window hasn't been opened in probably a few decades. Either it has swollen in the frame or it's been painted shut inside and I didn't notice. I have to throw my back into it before I get it to budge. The window groans and crackles like the brittle bones of a geriatric patient.

But I do it. I push the window up enough that I can climb through the opening. When I get inside, I close it again to keep the place warm.

As soon as I'm in the room, I turn on the flashlight. I keep the beam pointed downward, even though there isn't a single neighbor to notice anything suspicious. I take a long look around. Where does a person start looking for photographs in a room like this? The place is like an archive or something, crammed with books and papers and files. It's all the stuff the old man has been collecting his whole life.

The beam of my flashlight falls on the trunk, the one the old man keeps locked. Maybe that's where he keeps his more personal stuff—such as, for instance, some pictures he took way back when, pictures that prove my grandfather was a double agent. I try to lift the lid, thinking it would be nice if Curtis had left it open. But, of course, he hasn't.

So where's the key?

One idea that pops into my head right away: it's in the old man's pocket. Look at how he started locking his room after he found Katya inside. If I were him and afraid that someone might want to snoop around in my stuff, I'd definitely keep the keys with me at all times.

On the other hand…

I remember that when I got his glasses out of his bedside table, there was other stuff in there—odds and ends, the kinds of things people throw into junk drawers and forget about. Or the kinds of things they like to keep close. And I think, if he's got the key to his room in his pocket, why would he need to take the key to the trunk with him?

I go back to the bedside table, open the drawer and shine the flashlight inside.

I don't see a key.

But I do see a small leather book with black paper in it. I know right away what it is, because my grandmother has one just like it that was left to her by an aunt of hers. It's an old-fashioned photograph album. I take it out and flip it open. It's filled with black-and-white pictures. Each picture is mounted to the page by little black corners, and under each photo someone has written in silver ink, which is what my grandmother tells me people used to do.

The writing isn't in English. I think it's German, but I could be wrong. I don't have time to give it much thought or even to flip through the pictures. I don't have time to look at the papers that are folded in between a couple of album pages either.

I hear something, and I freeze.

Someone is unlocking the front door.

I tuck the photo album under my shirt, switch off my flashlight and head for the window. Once I'm there, I hesitate. The window made a lot of noise when I opened it. If I open it now, whoever is out there will hear me. Better to stick where I am and hope that whoever it is won't come in here. I figure it's a pretty safe bet, unless Curtis has forgotten something and has given Eric or Gerry the key to come back and get it for him.

Turns out I'm wrong.

Footsteps come toward the old man's door and then stop. Someone jiggles the doorknob.

"It's locked," a voice says. Katya. "He started locking it."

"Let me see." That's Noah. The doorknob rattles again. "Shouldn't be too hard," he says. I hear another sound. Something jingling.

"What's that?"

"It's a door opener."

"I've never seen anything like that before."

"It's a frat-house staple," Noah says. "You can't believe what we've got into with this thing. You can't believe what you can find behind locked doors in university buildings."

I scramble into the closet.

I hear another sound.

"There."

The door opens and light streams in from the hallway.

I'm crouched in the closet and praying that whatever they came to get isn't in here with me, because I will have one heck of a time explaining how I got into the house, never mind the locked room.

"Maybe you should call the restaurant," Katya says. "Ask them to tell Uncle Gerry we're running a little late."

"You do it," Noah says. "The number's in there. Selwyns."

I guess he's handed over his cell phone because a minute later I hear Katya asking to speak to the maître d'. She says that she and Mr. Green are running late and could he please tell her family and take their drinks order? She has a pleasant phone voice.

"So, where do we start?" she says once that's done.

Noah has turned on the lights in the room, and he's looking around. For a moment he doesn't speak. Then: "Geez, there's a lot of stuff in here."

"It drives Uncle Gerry crazy," Katya says. "He says all this paper makes the place a fire trap. But it's Grandpa's house…" Her voice trails off. "Are you sure about this, Noah?"

"Sure as I can be. My grandfather saw him, Katya. He saw Waldmann. He swears it was him. I showed you the picture."

"I know, but—"

"He looks just like your grandfather. And then when you showed me that picture of your grandfather and *his* father—there's no mistake, Katya. It's Waldmann."

Now I'm thinking fast. Waldmann is the Nazi who ran the concentration camp Noah's grandfather was in. Noah mentioned him the first time he was at the house. When Gerry gave Noah a hard time about his grandfather changing his name, Noah asked Gerry about *his* grandfather—did *he* change *his* name?

Now it sounds as if Noah thinks he did. It sounds as if Noah thinks Waldmann was the old man's father. That's crazy—isn't it?

But suppose it isn't.

Suppose Noah is right. That could mean the picture Adam sent me is of the same guy. Waldmann. It makes sense. If he was a notorious Nazi, and if he did the things Noah says he did, the Americans and the British would have wanted him to stand trial for war crimes. What if he managed to escape instead, like Eichmann? For sure he would have changed his name. Franken was probably his alias, just like Adler was David McLean's pseudonym.

I hear a snuffling sound, like someone starting to cry.

"Katya, it has nothing to do with your grandfather. He was just a kid at the time."

"What if he was in the Hitler Youth or something?"

"All German kids had to be in the Hitler Youth. They had no choice. They had to do what they were told. He seems like an okay guy, Katya. I bet he doesn't even know all the stuff his father did."

I think of all the books in there. All the files. All the magazines and journals. I have the impression that even if Curtis didn't know about it then, he probably knows now. He knows everything there is to know about the Nazis. Maybe he's interested because he's a collector. Maybe he's a closet Nazi. Or maybe he's interested because of what his father did. I know if my old man turned out to be someone like this Waldmann, I'd want to figure out why. Why would anyone do what he did?

I hear the two of them clattering around. Pretty soon Noah gets to the trunk.

"What's in here?" he asks.

"I don't know. It's locked," Katya says.

"There must be a key."

I peek through a tiny crack between the closet door and the doorframe.

Noah is looking around, as if he expects to see the key lying in plain sight. Then he reaches over the trunk. He gets hold of the massive framed photo of Hitler and lifts it up and over the trunk. He holds it up so he can get a good look at it.

"*Lieben Fritz*," he reads. "Fritz is a nickname for Friedrich. You see? I'm right. I knew it. I bet Hitler autographed this to your great-grandfather, Friedrich Waldmann."

Katya stares at it. She doesn't speak.

Noah turns the frame around. "Someone's tampered with it."

"That was me," Katya says. "I dropped it when I was in here last time. Grandpa heard me and—" She stops.

Noah has set down the picture and is crouching in front of it.

"I think there's something there," he says.

He digs in his pocket and uses whatever he pulls out—a penknife, maybe—to get the back off the photo. I hear a sharp intake of breath.

"Jackpot," he says.

"What is it?"

He holds up something. I can't see what it is.

"Look at this."

Katya bends down.

"I knew it," Noah says. "It's just like my grandfather said—he said they were all crooks and that they all stashed their stuff in the same place. Come on. Help me get this picture out of here."

"No!" Katya's cry surprises us both. "If you take the picture, Grandpa will miss it right away. I want to get this done before anyone suspects anything. I want it over with, Noah. And then I want us to go back to Boston. And I want Eric to come with us. You promised you'd help me with that."

"I will." Noah sounds distracted. I take another look, and I realize he's writing something down. When he finishes, he replaces the back of the photo and returns the picture to where he found it. "Come on," he says. "They're waiting. We'll have dinner. When we're finished, I'll make my excuses. You see everyone off and then come to meet me, just like we planned. Okay?"

Katya is sniffling again.

"Sweetheart, I'm not blaming your grandfather. But you said you wanted to do this, and it's the right thing. You know it."

He puts his arm around her and guides her out of the room. I hear another sound—Noah fiddling with the lock so Curtis won't come home to find his room's been broken into. Then I hear footsteps. Then silence. They're gone.

I wait a few minutes, just to be sure.

When everything stays quiet, I leave the closet and switch on my flashlight. I get the Hitler photo out from behind the trunk and pry the back off. I see writing. It's in German, I think, in some weird, old-style writing that would make it hard to read even if I understood the language, which I don't. Then I see the imprint of something on the back of the photographic paper, something that looks like it's been pressed in there between the back of the photo and the frame for a long time. Maybe for nearly seventy years.

It's the imprint of a key.

A small key.

It's way down in the corner, where it would have been hidden by the frame.

The key itself is missing.

The obvious question pops into my mind: the key to what?

It must have something to do with what Noah's grandfather said—crooks stashing their stuff. Did he mean Nazi crooks?

I take the photo of Mr. Sieg Heil—I don't care if the old man misses it. I roll it up as best I can and slide it under my jacket. Then I shove the window open and get out of there.

I go straight to Jacques's café. It's the only destination I can think of.

Jacques is there, but he's closing for the night, so I have to knock to get his attention. He lets me in and locks up after me.

"We're going to a party," he says, pouring me a drink of something. It turns out to be rum. I almost choke on it. "You come with us. Good food, good music."

"I can't."

"It's an African party," Elsie says. She tips her glass to Jacques and takes a sip. "When Jacques says good music, he means it's got a beat you can really dance to—you know what I mean?"

I don't even try to understand. I'm thinking about that key.

"What's wrong?" Elsie says. That's when I realize I've been staring at her.

"You know languages, right?" I say.

"Sure."

"Is German one of the ones you know?"

She nods.

I reach up under my jacket and shirt and pull out the rolled-up Hitler. She and Jacques both look surprised when they see it.

"That signature," Jacques says. "Is it real?"

"So they say." I hand the photo to Elsie. "There's writing on the back. I'm pretty sure it's German. Can you tell me what it says?"

She puts down her glass and fumbles under her little waitress apron for a pair of glasses. They have heavy black frames, and when she puts them on, she looks like a professor.

"It's the old-fashioned style of writing," she says. "It doesn't say much. It's the name of a bank and a number. Whoever wrote it wrote out the numbers."

Elsie shows me the name of the bank. It turns out it's in Switzerland, which I know from maybe a million old movies was supposedly neutral during the war. I also know from more recent information that it wasn't as neutral as it pretended to be. Swiss bankers helped a lot of Nazi types hide things—money and other valuables—and they knew what they were doing.

"Maybe it's an account number," she says.

"There was a key," I tell her.

"Then it must be a safe-deposit box," Jacques chimes in. "What's going on, *mon ami*? What's in the box?"

I tell him the truth. "I don't know for sure."

Something else occurs to me.

"Someone told me that Adler is German for eagle."

"That's right," Elsie says.

"What about Waldmann? Does that mean anything?"

"Waldmann?" She shrugs. "It's a common name. It's one of those occupation names."

"Occupation? You mean like when the Germans occupied Europe?"

She shakes her head. "In English, they're names like Baker or Carpenter or Fisher. They identified what people did for a living."

"And Waldmann?"

"It's the same kind of name, only in German."

"What does it mean?"

"It's a guy who probably took care of some noble-man's forest—you know, making sure the peas-ants didn't make off with wood and stuff. I guess in English the equivalent would be something like Forrester."

Waldmann equals Forrester, just like Adler equals eagle. What do you know? Everything is coming together, and it definitely involves David McLean.

I tuck *Der Führer* back up under my shirt. "I gotta go. Thanks for the information," I say to Elsie. And to Jacques: "And the drink."

Jacques reaches for a takeout menu and plucks a pen from Elsie's apron pocket. He writes something in the white space on the back of the menu.

"This is where the party is. Come when you can. We'll be there most of the night."

I rip off the corner with the address on it and shove it into my jeans pocket. I ask one last question.

"Do you know a restaurant called Selwyns?"

He nods.

"You know how to get there from here?"

He gives me directions. Then he unlocks the door for me and wishes me good luck.

I'm going to need it.

FOURTEEN

I see Gerry's rusted old truck in the parking lot at Selwyns. They're still in there. I scan the street for someplace warm where I can wait. It's a lot colder out now, and I'm starting to dream about the down-filled parka hanging in my closet back home. I'd give anything to be able to slide into it right now.

Plenty of stores and a few other restaurants have a good view of Selwyns's front door. Unfortunately, none of them look like the kind of place that would welcome someone as grubby-looking as me, whose sole purpose is to hang out. I cross the street and huddle next to a utility pole that cuts some, but not all, of the wind. While I wait—and freeze—my eyes shift back and forth between the restaurant door and the photos in the album I swiped from the old man's room. I check out the papers too. They're letters. Two of them. One from a congressman, the second from the State Department. *Proof*, the old man said. He has it. Boy, does he have it!

I tuck everything back up under my sweatshirt and anchor it in the waistband of my jeans. I hope the Forrester family isn't going to spend all night in that restaurant.

They don't. But by the time the restaurant door opens to let someone out, I'm shivering uncontrollably.

It's Noah.

I hope he doesn't get into a car or flag a taxi.

I hope in vain.

He hands a ticket to the uniformed guy at the door, who trots to the parking lot, returns a few minutes later in a car and jumps out to let Noah in, but not before sticking out his hand for a tip. I look around for a cab. There aren't any. All I can do is stand in the dark, shivering, while I watch Noah's car disappear from sight.

Ten minutes pass, then ten more. I begin not to care about the key or Waldmann or how or even whether

David McLean was responsible for him dying in a Soviet labor camp. If the guy was a Nazi, then he deserved it. I begin to wonder why I'm standing here. Someone just shot at me. Again. And killed someone else. Again. And I was right there both times. Either of those bodies could have been mine. My grandma could be coming down here to identify me in a morgue instead of to sign a bunch of papers that amount to a promise-to-appear in a murder case—assuming an arrest is ever made and assuming that Carver, after the latest shooting, feels inclined to let me leave the country.

The restaurant door opens again. The guy in the uniform accepts the ticket Gerry hands him while Katya helps the old man get his walker over the little bump at the door. Eric comes out, hunched deep in his jacket.

The truck rattles to the front of the restaurant. When the valet approaches Gerry, I see that he doesn't bother to hold out his hand, but Gerry defies expectations and slips him some bills. I see a look of surprise—pleasant surprise—on the valet's face. Gerry must have enjoyed his dinner.

Katya helps Curtis into the truck. Eric puts his walker in the back and climbs in beside him. Katya and

Gerry stand on the sidewalk, talking. I see Katya shake her head. Finally, Gerry kisses her on the cheek and gets in behind the wheel. The truck drives away.

Katya puts up the collar of her coat against the wind. What's she going to do? Call a cab? There's nothing much on the street. Maybe she got the valet guy to call one for her.

But no—she starts walking. *Thank you!*

She marches briskly down the block. I trail her, keeping to the other side of the street and hanging back far enough that I hope she won't notice me.

She doesn't look around. She keeps walking, head down, shoulders rounded, exposing as little of herself as possible as she heads into the wind. I keep her in sight.

Five minutes later she turns up the walk to a small house on a desolate street. It's completely dark, no streetlights, no Christmas lights, no nothing. It's hard to picture this place as a once-thriving community with people and kids and snowmen in front yards and Christmas trees visible through living-room windows.

Katya goes around the side of the house. I walk past and hide in the shadows, which is easy because of the streetlight shortage. She opens the door and goes inside. A light fills one window.

I wait a little longer, but nothing happens. I think about what to do. Katya is here to meet Noah—that much I know. If he shows up in his car and they take off together, that'll be the end of it. I will have gone through all of this for one very large goose egg.

I walk to the door.

It's unlocked.

I open it and step into a small landing. To my left are stairs down into a basement. Straight ahead, up two steps, is another door.

I open it and see a dark hallway. To my right, toward the back of the house, there's light.

The place isn't much. The paint is a kind of beige that—I'm just guessing here—was white thirty or forty or so years ago when it was first applied and, like some fading movie star, hasn't aged well. The floor is hardwood. I know because I can see lengths of scuffed wood in the places where the scarred checker-board linoleum has broken away. I creep to the back of the house, and peek into the room where there's light. The furniture—a little table, a couch, a couple of easy chairs—all seems to predate the paint on the walls. Either that or it's been living fast and hard and has grown old before its time.

"How long do you think we'll be gone?" It's Katya. I follow her voice. She's in the living room, sitting on the couch, which now that I see it up close, has stuffing leaking out of most of its cushions. She still has her hat on. Her purse is on her lap. I can see her breath in front of her face. Noah is in front of the fireplace in his coat, silk scarf and thin leather gloves. I didn't see his car outside. Maybe he parked around the back. He's holding a sheet of notebook paper, and he's reading it. He's smiling.

"We did it," he says. "I had to pinch myself to stop from smiling all through dinner."

"I smiled anyway," Katya says. She's still smiling now. "We're engaged. We're allowed to smile."

But her smile evaporates faster than spit on summer asphalt when she sees me.

"What are you doing here?" Her eyes practically bug out of her head. Not only is she wondering what I'm doing here, but I bet she's also wondering how I managed to find her.

Noah is surprised too. He tenses up and looks around warily—wondering, I suppose, if I'm alone or if someone has come with me.

"I don't want to keep you," I say, nice and friendly. "You two are about to leave town, right? Switzerland?"

Katya's eyes snap to Noah. His smile is taut, like a well-wound spring. Or like a bowstring armed with an arrow and drawn back, ready to shoot.

"Where we go and what we do is none of your business," Katya informs me.

Okay. "How about your grandfather? Is it his business?"

"What do you want?" Noah demands. There's no doubt in his mind that I'm here for something. It's a good thing it's not the key I'm after, because I have a feeling Noah isn't about to let that slip through his fingers.

"I just want to ask Katya a few questions. That's it. I don't care about the key."

It's true. I don't. Why should I?

Noah's eyes don't waver from me. He wants me gone, the sooner the better. "What do you know about the key?"

I turn to Katya.

"I know about your great-grandfather," I say. But that isn't right. "I mean, I know who he was.

But what I don't know is how or why my grandfather was involved. Do you?" I'm hoping that if she's done her research—or Noah has done his—they'll know exactly what happened to him.

"*Your* grandfather?" She's confused. "What does *your* grandfather have to do with anything?"

"My question exactly." I tell her about the old newspaper photograph of Friedrich Waldmann, and then I tell her about David McLean—about what I've been able to find out, which is mostly just him showing up in Buenos Aires to offer her great-grandfather a job. I also tell her about Mirella.

"That's the Mirella you were asking about?" she says. "She was married to my great-grandfather?"

"Apparently. She sent a postcard from your grandfather's address to some neighbors back home. They never heard from her after that. She got a job here. I guess she made a new life."

"So that's how my grandpa knew her." She digests that. "He never said anything about her. He never said anything about his father either. I never knew a thing about him until two months ago." She slumps down into the couch again and looks me over. "He was a horrible man."

"He ran a concentration camp," I say. "Like Noah said." I glance at him. "Isn't that right, Noah?"

Noah stares at me. I imagine him as a prosecutor, a district attorney, with an accused murderer on the stand. I imagine him grilling that person.

"I read about him after Noah told me who he was," Katya says. "I read everything I could find. He was notorious. Not exactly Mengele, but a terrible man. He ran away after the war to avoid getting captured by the Allies and having to stand trial. He hid out for the rest of his life. My grandfather was a boy at the time of the war. Noah says he probably didn't know everything that was going on, and even if he did, there was probably nothing he could do about it. He was probably brainwashed."

Maybe, I think. Maybe not.

"That's why my grandfather changed his name," she says. "It's why he never talked about his past."

"He collected a lot of stuff about the Nazis," I say.

"We think—Noah and I think—that he was trying to understand them. You know, so that he could understand his own father."

Maybe, I think. Maybe not.

"Noah's grandfather was in Waldmann's camp," Katya says. "He survived. He told Noah all about what happened there. And then, years later, Noah's grandfather saw my great-grandfather. He recognized him. He told Noah everything about him. When Noah met me and saw the picture of my grandpa and great-grandpa from when Grandpa was a boy, he almost fainted. I'm not kidding—his face turned white. When he told me why, I couldn't believe it. I didn't want to believe it. My great-grandfather was a mass murderer. He was a criminal. And I never knew."

What do you say to something like that?

I turn to Noah. "So your grandfather saw Waldmann and recognized him."

Noah nods. It's a tight move, quick, with no emotion behind it except maybe a firm desire to get me gone.

"He spotted him in Mexico," Katya says. "When he was on holiday. I keep thinking, what if he hadn't taken that holiday? What if he hadn't spotted Waldmann? Would I ever have found out the truth about my family?"

"Katya, we don't have time for this. And you don't have to explain anything to him," Noah says.

"I'm not ashamed, Noah. That's what this is all about, isn't it? I'm not ashamed. I just want to do the right thing." She looks at me. "It happened when Noah was just a kid. After that, Noah's grandfather tried to track down Waldmann. But he died without ever seeing him again." I notice that she's trying to avoid describing him as her great-grandfather.

I think about what Carver would call this story—cockamamie.

"That's impossible," I say. I guess I sound hard-hearted, because Katya stares at me in shock. "What I mean," I say, "is that Noah's grandfather didn't see Waldmann in Mexico. He couldn't have."

"What do you mean? Of course he did." Katya glances at Noah for confirmation. "That's how I know what I know."

I unzip my jacket and start to reach up under my sweatshirt. Noah flinches. That should have told me something, but it didn't.

I pull out the small leather-bound photo album and extract the two sheets of paper from its pages. I hand them to Katya. She skims the first one and frowns.

"Who's Heinrich Franken?"

"That's the phony name Waldmann used when he fled to Argentina," I say. "It sounds to me like the Americans used it too. I guess they didn't want anyone to know what they were doing."

"Argentina?" She frowns. She's still frowning as she reads further.

"The first letter is from a congressman from California," I tell Noah. "The American government offered Franken or Waldmann or whatever you want to call him—Katya's great-grandfather—a job. Curtis and Mirella came up first with the family belongings. Franken was supposed to follow. He never showed up. It took Curtis and Mirella two months to find out what happened. They got that letter and then a visit from a government official. They were told that Franken had been kidnapped by the Russians."

Katya is wide-eyed as she starts in on the second letter.

"The second one is even better," I tell Noah. "It's from the State Department. Apparently, Mirella and Curtis kept after them to get Franken back. That's the answer they finally got. It says that Franken—Waldmann—died in a Soviet labor camp shortly after he arrived there. Way before you were born. You want to show him the letters, Katya?"

"So maybe my grandfather made a mistake about the time," Noah says. "Maybe he saw him earlier."

"Thirty years earlier? That's some mistake," I say. "Especially for a guy who's so good at remembering things like faces."

"What difference does it make?" Noah says. "It doesn't make any difference. He saw him and knew it was Waldmann."

And a crook, I think. That's what Noah said his grandfather told him: *They were all crooks, and they all stashed their stuff in the same place.*

"What's in that Swiss bank, Katya?"

Noah answers for her. "That's none of your business."

"I told you, Noah. I'm not ashamed." Katya looks steadily at him. "It's gold and jewelry, all of it stolen." She doesn't say who it was stolen from. She doesn't have to.

"So Waldmann was also a thief," I say.

Katya bows her head. She nods.

"A thief with a fortune tucked away in a Swiss bank account that I bet you can't wait to get your hands on." I'm looking at Noah when I say that. His expression is stony. It's Katya who takes offense.

"We're not doing this for ourselves. We're going to give it back."

"Back? To whom? All the people he stole from are long gone. Most of their families are gone too," I say.

"To a good cause. To help people." I can see she means it. "After what Waldmann did, it's the least I can do."

"So why the secrecy? Why didn't you tell your grandfather or your uncle what you're up to?"

She bites her lip. "Noah said it would be better to just do it. Things have been so tough at home. If Uncle Gerry knew about that safe-deposit box…" Her voice trails off.

I get it. She wants to make sure no one is tempted. She really seems to want to do the right thing—with no interference. I have to give her credit for that.

Noah pushes away from the fireplace. "Come on, Katya. We have to go."

When he turns to pick something up from the fireplace mantel, Katya looks past me and frowns again. That's when I hear a floorboard creak. I think Noah does too, because we both turn at the same time.

There's someone else in the room.

It's Ed Mitron. I'm confused. What's *he* doing here? Did my grandmother call him? Is he looking for me? If he is, how did he manage to find me? And why does he look like that—in a long overcoat, both hands behind his back in a casual pose, like a man waiting for a bus?

"Who—?" Katya begins, then breaks off.

Mitron nods pleasantly at me and then looks to Noah.

"What are you doing here?" Noah demands.

Not "Who are you?" but "What are you doing here?" Noah knows him. He knows Mitron. I start to get a bad feeling.

Katya's eyes search out Noah's. "What's going on? Who is this man?" She swings around to Mitron. "Who are you?"

"That doesn't matter, my dear," Mitron says. He turns to Noah. "You have the key and the information?"

Noah holds up an envelope. "What are you doing here, Ed? I have everything under control."

Mitron answers by bringing one hand from around his back and raising it. He's holding a gun.

"Give the envelope to the girl, Noah," he says.

Noah's eyes are on the gun. When they finally flick up to Mitron's eyes, I see acceptance. Or maybe confirmation. I'm not sure which. He hands the envelope to Katya.

"What are you doing here?" I ask Mitron. "Did you follow me?" It's the only explanation I can think of.

"Follow *you*?" He shakes his head. "No. Not at all. In fact, I was disheartened when I got your note. It was never my intention to involve you, not if I didn't have to. And I sincerely hoped I didn't, Rennie. For your father's sake."

"Ed—" Noah begins.

Mitron ignores him. "You were at my house for ten days, you and your father, and we had a pleasant time, did we not? I was beginning to think that I had been wrong."

Wrong? I don't understand.

"I was beginning to think you knew nothing. But that last day, for the first time since you arrived, you asked to use the Internet. The next thing I knew, you were off to see a friend in Argentina. Naturally, I had to know what that was about. And then when I heard you were headed for Detroit…"

"What?" I say. "How did you know that?"

Mitron just smiles. I'm totally confused. And then it hits me.

"The guy who pulled me off the plane in Miami—you know him, don't you?"

I get another smile from Mitron, this one cryptic. Yeah, Mitron knows the guy all right. That's why I got pulled aside. That's why I got questioned. But why? What's Mitron's angle? He's supposed to be a good guy, isn't he? The Major worships him.

"Why are you here?" I ask him.

He glances at his watch again. What's he waiting for? Or maybe the question is, who is he waiting for?

"The real question, Rennie," Mitron says, "is what you are doing here. It would have been so much easier, so much better for everyone, including your father, if you had simply gone back to Canada where you belong."

When I was little, I used to do stuff my grandma didn't understand, usually dumb stuff that drove her crazy. She used to ask, "*Why on earth would you want to do something like that, Rennie?*" I'd pretty much give her the same answer every time: "*I dunno.*" And she'd sigh and say I was a riddle, wrapped in a mystery, inside an enigma. It was something a guy named Winston Churchill said once, and my grandma said it "*described* me *to a T*."

It also describes Mitron. Every time he opens his mouth, things get more puzzling. I guess my expression makes that point.

"I didn't follow you here, Rennie. I was going to come one way or another."

Noah stirs. "You said—" He stops when Mitron waves the gun at him.

"What do you mean, *he* said?" Katya wants to know. "Noah?"

Noah refuses to look at her.

Mitron continues talking to me. "Your grandfather and I crossed paths once before, a long time ago."

That was news to me.

"My father was in the government of Juan Péron. You know who he was, Rennie?"

Yeah, I know. He was president of Argentina back then. My grandma insisted I watch the movie *Evita* with her—Madonna as Péron's wife, Eva. I hated the whole thing from start to finish, but I didn't tell Grandma. She belted out "Don't Cry for Me, Argentina" right along with the Material Girl.

"Péron welcomed ex-Nazis with open arms. He thought they could help him with some of his domestic problems. That's why there was such a large German population in Argentina after the war. Eichmann was there. So was Waldmann. He lived under an alias, but he was found out back in the 1960s. Your grandfather was sent down to bring him to America. He claimed he was ambushed and that Waldmann was taken from him—by the Russians, he said. It seemed plausible enough. The Russians were as interested in Waldmann as the Americans were, maybe more so."

"Why would they be interested in an ex-Nazi?" I asked. "To make him stand trial for what he did?"

"Because he developed a biological weapon. It was reputed to be the most efficient biological weapon ever developed. It was highly virulent, extremely effective at a low dosage, easy to transport, easy to use, capable of neutralizing up to a few thousand square kilometers. Everything you could want in such a weapon. And this is the important part, Rennie— he also developed the vaccine to protect against it. The Americans wanted it. So did the Russians."

I'm staring at him, trying to imagine why my grandfather would agree to have anything to do with Waldmann and his weapon.

"The Russians never denied that they had taken Waldmann. In fact, I believe they made it known to the Americans that he had died in one of their camps." He shakes his head. "They must have enjoyed the game. They must have laughed at how afraid the Americans were when they learned that Waldmann and his secrets had fallen into Russian hands. But these things happen. It's part of the game."

Some game, I thought.

"I didn't think about Waldmann again—until I heard about your grandfather's death and the missions he devised for you and your cousins. That tickled my memory. Things have changed in Russia now, Rennie. It's much easier to get information if you have the right contacts and can pay for it. Even the Kremlin has started to open its archives. I wondered what had happened to Waldmann's secrets. So I made inquiries." He shakes his head again. "And do you know what I found out? The Russians never had him."

"What?" I say. "You think Waldmann is still alive?"

He laughed. "That would be a neat trick. He would be well over a hundred years old if he were. No, I don't think he's alive. And now I know the Russians never had him, despite what the Americans said. My sources tell me that the Americans never got their hands on him either and that they genuinely believed the Russians had him. That's what they told the family. I suspect that something went wrong and he never made it out of Argentina."

Katya goes still. "Then it's possible that Noah's grandfather saw him in Mexico," she says softly.

"Noah's grandfather?" Mitron chuckles. "Believe as you wish," he says, "but give me that envelope so that I can be on my way."

Katya doesn't move.

"Give it to him, Katya," I say.

"Do it, Katya," Noah says.

Katya refuses. "It's not his."

"It's not yours either, my dear," Mitron says. "So, please." He extends a hand.

I look into his eyes. There's no hesitation there.

"Do it," I say to Katya. "Whatever your great-grandfather did, it's not worth dying for."

"He's right, Katya," Noah says. "Give him the envelope."

Mitron's hand is still extended.

Katya moves toward him.

A shot rings out. What the—? Then another.

Mitron buckles. He stares at Noah, at the gun in Noah's hand, and crumples to the floor.

Katya opens her mouth, but nothing comes out.

Noah turns the gun on me. The only thing that surprises me is how calm I am. Maybe it's like they say—you can get used to anything. And in this town, I'm getting used to people pointing guns at me.

Noah steps forward, his eyes and his gun still on me. He eases the envelope out of Katya's hand and slips it into his pocket.

"Katya, I need you to do something for me."

She turns wide-eyed to him.

"I need you to get that gun." He nods at the weapon in Mitron's hand.

She stares at him as if he's crazy. He wants her to touch a dead body? Her head starts to shake: no, no, no.

"Katya, listen to me. That man is a criminal. He just wanted the money, and he was ready to do anything to get it."

"Unlike you," I say.

He ignores me.

"Get the gun, Katya. Please."

Tears are rolling down Katya's cheeks.

"Please, darling. Then we can go."

"Noah lied to you, Katya," I tell her again. "His grandfather never saw Waldmann. You heard what Mitron said."

"He was the one who was lying," Noah says. "He was trying to confuse you, Katya." He puts an arm around her. "I love you, Katya. You know that. Give me that gun and then we can go. Remember our plan? It's what you wanted to do, right? We can go. We can take care of everything. Then, when we come back, we can get Eric and take him back to Boston with us."

"He's lying, Katya."

"Shut up!" Noah glowers at me.

"What about him?" Katya asks. She's looking at Mitron.

"Don't worry about him. Just give me the gun."

"But why did you do it, Noah? Why did you shoot him?"

"Because he was going to hurt you. Katya, there are lots of men like him around. Treasure hunters.

He knew about your great-grandfather, didn't he? He knew about the safe-deposit box. He was going to take the envelope, and then he was going to hurt you. He had a gun, didn't he?"

She nods.

"Do as I say."

This time she does. She picks up the gun and hands it to him. I notice he hasn't taken off his gloves. I notice Katya isn't wearing any.

Noah points the gun at Mitron and fires again and again. Katya cowers, her hands clasped over her ears. Noah doesn't stop firing until he empties the gun. Then he holds it out to me.

"Take it."

I don't.

"Take it," he says again.

"Or what? Or you'll shoot me?"

"You can take it now or I can put it in your hand later. Your choice," he says.

Katya comes alive at that. "What are you going to do?"

"We're going to leave. But before we do, we're going to call the police and tell them where they can find a murderer. Do you have your phone, Katya? Make the call. I'll tell you what to say."

She's shaking her head again. I don't know how she thought this was all going to work out, but it's clear to me that she never imagined this.

"Call them and tell them you heard shots coming from this house."

"But Noah, you—"

"We'll be long gone by the time they get here."

I bet the plan is that I'll still be here.

"Make the call, Katya."

"Don't do it, Katya," I say. "Don't trust him."

"Shut up. Make the call, Katya."

"Your prints are already on Mitron's gun, Katya," I tell her. "Now he wants mine on them too. But he's wearing gloves and he's got the key to the safe-deposit box. He lied to you once. He's lying to you again."

Noah is on me like a flash. His hand darts out, and he hits me hard on the face with the gun. I reel backward. The pain is overpowering. I wonder if I'm going to lose any teeth.

"My car is outside," Noah says. "Go wait for me there. I'll make the call."

"What are you going to do?" Katya asks.

"I said, go wait in the car, Katya." His tone is sharp. Clearly, he's an in-charge guy, but the stunned look in Katya's eyes tells me that this way of speaking to her is something new.

"Katya, I just want to make sure he doesn't tell anyone anything until we're gone."

She picks up her purse and slips its strap over her shoulder.

"Ask him how he's going to do that, Katya," I say.

At first I think she's going to ignore me. But she doesn't. She's frowning when she turns to look at me.

"Go ahead," I say. "Ask him."

Noah wraps an arm around her shoulder and kisses her on the cheek. She melts against him.

"Go wait outside," he says softly. "Nothing bad is going to happen, I promise."

But she doesn't move. "Noah, did you know about my great-grandfather before you met me?"

"Of course I did. I told you that. My grandfather—"

"I mean, did you know he was *my* great-grandfather?"

"No. I told you that too, Katya." His voice is soft, reasonable. "But did I know about Waldmann? Yes, I did."

"Because your grandfather saw him?"

"That's right. That's what he told me, Katya. I swear it is."

"Then why did that man say Waldmann never made it out of Argentina? And those letters. They said that Waldmann died a long time ago."

"Did it ever occur to you that Mitron was lying?"

Katya's confused. I'm not.

"I know Mitron," I say. "He had no reason to lie to me. He was here to get that key. He knew what was in that box. Just like you and Noah did."

Noah's lips brush Katya's cheek. "Trust me, darling. Go wait for me in the car."

"Don't go, Katya. He's going to kill me. That's how he's going to make sure I don't say anything. Katya, he's holding a gun that has Mitron's prints on it. Mitron's and yours. Not his. Yours. He's going to kill me as soon as you're out of the house and—"

Noah hits me again. This time I fall to the floor. This time he's definitely broken something. This time

I hope it's a tooth, because that would be better than if it's my jaw.

"Get up," Noah says.

I struggle to my feet. There's blood in my mouth. I spit it out.

Katya starts to walk from the room. A look of triumph crosses Noah's face. He raises the gun. He's just itching to use it—I can see it in his eyes. He's looking forward to it. Nothing is going to stand between Noah and the treasure he's worked so hard to get.

Up comes the gun. It's pointed at my chest—the biggest and surest target, especially at that range. And I already know he can shoot.

He's waiting, listening for Katya to leave.

But she doesn't. Instead, she walks slowly back to Noah, swings her purse to get some leverage and hits him on the side of the head with it before he knows what's happening.

He lunges forward. The gun goes flying.

I dive for it.

I grab it and get up on my knees before Noah can recover. I hold the gun on him and pray he doesn't make me use it. I don't want to have to shoot anyone—ever.

Katya is the only one standing. Tears well in her eyes.

I think, I should call someone.

The only person I can think of is Detective Carver.

FIFTEEN

I'm in the police station again, in a small room with Carver, who is shaking his head. He's also recording every word I say.

"So about this cell phone," he says, nodding at the phone on the table between us. It's bagged and tagged as evidence. "Tell me again how you came to have it in your possession."

I tell him for the second time, or maybe the third. I don't stumble even once. Honesty is the best policy. It's also the easiest. You don't have to remember anything special. You just tell it like it is.

Carver shakes his head. "What a maroon," he says.

"A what?" What is he talking about?

"Eric. His buddy too. All this texting. They think they're so smart, and then they do dumb stuff. You can't believe how many times email or texting trips people up. They think just because they delete it, it's gone for good."

I know that already. "A maroon?"

Carver shrugs. "I grew up on Bugs Bunny. Maroon—that's his word for a moron. An idiot."

"Good word."

"So, we've got Eric for conspiring to kill you. He thought he had that all wrapped up with a bow— mysterious Spider Face kills only eyewitness to alley shooting. But he thought wrong. We can prove that, thanks to the texts on this phone. We also have him texting the owner of this cell phone where and when to be in that alley, which means we can make a second conspiracy-to-murder charge for Mitchell." He means Duane. "We also have his buddy, the guy who shot Duane, thanks to some other texts that led us to friends of his who decided it was in their best interest to cooperate with us. That spider tattoo— temporary, by the way—was intended to focus your attention enough to make you a viable eyewitness, and therefore a target later on, without giving you what you needed to make a solid identification."

"Smart."

"Smart for a couple of maroons. If we're lucky, maybe we can get a confession on the two college kids. It'd be nice for the parents. Eric and his pals are facing life for killing a cop. That might put them in the mood for a deal."

He looks across the table at me.

"You want to tell me again about this guy Mitron?"

I tell him everything I know. While I talk, I think about the Major. How is he going to react when he hears about this? Mitron was his mentor. He looked up to the man.

"The girl isn't disputing anything you told us," Carver says. "We've got the boyfriend locked up. His name isn't Noah Green, by the way. It's Thomas Elliot. He's descended from Irish immigrants. He never had a grandfather in a concentration camp."

"Did you tell Katya?"

He nods. "She took it hard."

"What about the safe-deposit box?"

"She handed over the key. She didn't have to, but she did. She doesn't want what's in the box. As far

248

as I can tell, she never did. She just wanted to make amends."

"But she didn't do anything."

Carver lets out a long sigh. "Family is a funny thing," he says. "It gets to you in ways you don't expect. When she found out about her great-grandfather, she says it made her feel evil, that just knowing she was related to a man like Friedrich Waldmann made her feel that she was part of it."

"But it's not true."

"True or not, she blames Waldmann for the way her brother turned out. Like I said, family is a funny thing. How we feel about ourselves—sometimes we don't get that just from the living. Sometimes we get it from the dead."

I think about my mother. I can't help it. When Carver says that, there she is. We're in that car together, driving through the Canadian Shield and past a sign that warns about falling rock. We're there because I pestered her to take me someplace she didn't want to go. That car ride was my very last trip with her. It's a long story, but I know that Carver's right. Sometimes we get as much from the dead as we do from the living. Sometimes more.

Another hour passes before Carver is finally done with me and I'm in the clear. He believes me when I tell him I'll come back when and if he needs me again. When I finally step out of the interview room, someone is waiting for me.

My grandma.

All of a sudden, I'm a little kid again. I run to her, almost bowling over a couple of uniforms, one of whom snarls, "Watch it, kid!" All I want is to throw myself at my grandma, who, in case I haven't mentioned it yet, is the coolest grandma in the world.

Then I see she isn't alone.

Ari is with her. Grandma notices my reaction.

"He drove me down," she says. "I was so worried, Rennie."

I embrace her and feel her arms wrap around me in a bear hug, emphasis on bear. Even at her age, Grandma still goes to the gym. She does a weights class. She jokes that the weights aren't as heavy as they used to be, but there's tone in her muscles. I can feel it under her heavy winter coat and what I am guessing is a thick wool sweater.

"Are you mad at me?" I ask.

She hugs me again, and that's my answer.

"I understand you're free to go," she says. "So what do you say we get out of here?"

Ari bundles us into the backseat of his car and takes us to a nice restaurant, for which I'm actually grateful. All of a sudden I'm ravenous. While we eat, I tell Grandma everything.

"Well, that explains that," she says.

"What?"

"Your father was surprised to hear from Ed Mitron after all those years."

I think about the Major. "He's going to be pretty upset when I tell him what happened."

"He's going to be relieved you're okay," Grandma says. "That's all he ever cares about, Rennie."

I open my mouth to argue with her. The Major? Relieved? I end up not saying a word. I hope she's right.

I pull out the little leather photo album and flip through the pages. Grandma is intrigued.

"Curtis, Katya's grandfather, says he took some pictures that prove David McLean—" I stop. "He says he took some pictures of David McLean."

And, sure enough, I find them. There are three of them. One shows my grandfather beaming as he shakes hand with Friedrich Waldmann, aka Heinrich Franken, who looks relaxed in casual clothes. He's standing in the street in front of the house I visited in Buenos Aires. There's a second picture, this one with David McLean, Waldmann and an attractive young woman. "That must be Mirella," I say. "Waldmann's wife."

"She looks too young." Grandma leans in for a closer look.

"She was only a year older than Waldmann's son," I tell her. "It's hard to imagine what she saw in Waldmann."

"Well, she looks happy enough. Maybe she just wanted to go to the United States." She points to another picture. "Well, look at that."

I look. It's a picture that clearly Curtis didn't take, because he's in it. It's a photo of him and Mirella. Mirella is smiling at the camera as she holds up a map of the United States and points to its west coast. Her expression seems to say: *Look at this! This is where I'm going!*

Curtis shows no interest in the map. He's staring at her.

"If you ask me," Grandma says, "that young man is in love with that young woman. Look at the expression on his face. Your grandfather used to look at me like that, Rennie."

I'm stunned when she blushes. Boy, you never know about old people. It's so hard to imagine them as young, but once upon a time they surely were. Curtis is right—how much does one generation really know about the one before it? I look at the picture again, and I see what my grandmother sees.

I take a look at another picture with David McLean in it. It's similar to the first one—David McLean and Friedrich Waldmann shaking hands and smiling—and I'm trying to figure out if McLean's smile is genuine or not when something catches me eye. There's someone else there, almost out of the frame. A passerby—at least, that's what he looks like at first. Until I recognize him. I pick up the album for a closer look. Grandma frowns.

"Rennie?"

I show her the picture, pointing to the passerby.

Grandma looks at Ari. So do I. The only difference between the two of us is that I'm surprised.

"That's you." I push the album across the table at Ari and point to the young man at the end of the street, the man who looks like he's just passing through.

Ari glances at the picture. He and Grandma exchange looks. Then Grandma gently pats her mouth with a corner of her linen napkin. She excuses herself and makes her way across the carpeted floor toward the hallway that leads to the washrooms. I watch her go. Ari takes a sip of his water.

"Did your grandmother ever tell you how we met?" he asks.

"No." And to tell the truth, I don't particularly care.

"It was when I was with Mossad."

"Mossad?" He's kidding, right? "The Israeli secret service?"

He nods. "My parents met right after the war, in a camp for displaced persons. They were both the only survivors of their families. I was born in that camp and raised in Israel. As soon as I was old enough, I joined the Israeli army. From there I was recruited by Mossad. Naturally, I had a special interest in bringing fugitive Nazis to justice."

"You went after Waldmann too?" I look at the white-haired man across the table, his face tanned and deeply lined, his wild old-man eyebrows shooting out in all directions, his stomach straining a little too much against the buttons of his crisp shirt.

It's hard to imagine him in the army, let alone as some kind of secret agent.

"The Americans wanted Waldmann very badly. They were interested in developing weapons that would give them an edge over the Soviets. And Waldmann was reputed to be an expert in biological warfare. He had a file that contained all his notes and formulas. Of course, they didn't tell David that. Instead, they told him that Waldmann had to be brought to justice, called to account for what he had done during the war. They asked David to go down there to ensure he got safely out of Argentina and back to America."

"But why him? Was he working for the CIA?"

"I only know what he told me."

"Which is?"

"An old friend at the Pentagon asked for his help."

"Why?"

"Your grandfather knew Waldmann."

"What do you mean? How?"

"They met after the war, when David was in the import/export business. It took him to South America regularly, and that's where he met Waldmann. At a café, I think it was, studying a book on chess.

David spoke excellent German, and he struck up a conversation with Waldmann—who at the time was going by the name Franken. Of course, he didn't know who Waldmann was. And as I understand it, Waldmann claimed to have immigrated to Argentina before the war. I believe he even had papers to prove it. When his true identity came to light, the Americans thought they would have a better chance with him if he were approached by someone he already knew."

Maybe that made sense. "But why the alias? He had an Argentinian passport under the name Klaus Adler."

"It was all very hush-hush. The Americans didn't want to raise any red flags. Waldmann wasn't the only ex-Nazi in Argentina, you know. They wanted to get Waldmann out of the country quietly. Your grandfather also had false papers for Waldmann, who would be traveling in disguise. The two of them would be just two Argentinian citizens of German descent traveling in South America. Once out of the country, they would fly back to Washington."

"Hush-hush? But his wife told the neighbors—"

Ari sighs. "Waldmann was less than discreet. He was a boastful man and proud of being recruited by the Americans. Perhaps if he had been more circum-spect, things might have turned out differently."

"What do you mean?"

"The Americans weren't the only ones interested in Waldmann."

"You mean the Russians, right?"

"Among others."

"Among others?" I look at Ari. "Mossad wanted him too," I say. "*You* wanted him."

Ari's eyes turn as hard as diamonds. "My mother's family—her parents, her sisters, her brother—they all died in his camp. You bet I wanted him." He gaze drifts away for a moment. He reaches for his glass and takes another sip. Then, drawing in a deep breath, he continues.

"David was instructed to offer Waldmann a job. Naturally, Waldmann leapt at the opportunity. But at the last minute Waldmann let it slip that he knew the Americans wanted him because of the research he had done on biological weapons. At the time, the Americans were very keen on getting and maintaining a military edge over the Soviets. David didn't know this about Waldmann. I don't know what he would have done if I hadn't showed up."

"What do you mean?"

"I was watching him—and Waldmann. A comrade and I…shall we say…*intercepted* their car on the way to the border."

"You were going to kidnap Waldmann?"

"The Americans didn't care if Waldmann was ever called to account for his war crimes. We did. We were going to see to it that he paid for what he had done."

"So you hijacked David McLean." I peer into those flesh-pocketed eyes and try to imagine the scene— my grandfather and this old man, both young, both determined, both doing what they saw as their duty.

Ari sighs. "That was the plan. Unfortunately, we hit a snag."

"What do you mean?"

"I told you the Americans weren't the only ones who were interested. The Russians got wind of him. I'm not sure how. It took us and the Americans a long time to track him down. And once the Americans found him, they were cautious. I have no idea how the Russians knew where Waldmann was, let alone how they knew where and when the Americans were taking him out of the country. But they found out.

They got to your grandfather and Waldmann before we could. They ambushed them outside of the city."

"So the Russians really did take Waldmann from my grandfather? That's really true?"

"No," Ari said. "It's not."

"Then what happened to him?"

"The Russians took him from David before we got to them. When they tried to handcuff him to get him into their truck, Waldmann fought like a demon. I think he knew what was in store for him. The Russians were harder on Nazis than the Americans. A lot harder. Waldmann managed to get free. I thought he would make a run for it, but that isn't what happened."

"*You* got to him?"

Ari shakes his head. "Like many of his fellows, Waldmann was a coward. He knew what the Russians would do to him once they had his secrets. He got a gun away from one of his captors, and he killed himself."

I stare at him.

"You look exactly like those Russian agents did when they saw him pull the trigger. But there was nothing they could do. It was too late."

"So what happened?"

"I don't know what they told their superiors. But naturally, they wanted to get rid of any evidence of their failure. That meant eliminating David. Fortunately for him, that didn't go according to plan either," Ari said.

I stared at him. I knew my grandfather had been through a lot, but I'd had no idea how much. I tried to imagine what it must have felt like to face the Russians and know he was going to die.

"You stopped them, didn't you?"

"My comrade and I, yes. We buried Waldmann. David told the Americans that the Russians had taken him. It was true as far as it went. The Russians, I suppose, would have blamed Mossad."

"What happened to Waldmann's file?"

"There was no file."

"How do you know?"

"Because Waldmann told David. He boasted that he knew someone would pay him for what he had in his head—the results of all his experiments. His supposed secret weapon."

"Supposed? You don't think he really had one?"

Ari shrugs. "Whether he did or he didn't, it became a moot point when he pulled the trigger. The matter was finished. But I think maybe David got a little satisfaction when he thought about the Americans sweating because they thought the Russians had Waldmann. And, of course, the Russians didn't deny it. They would look like fools if they admitted he'd killed himself in front of their agents."

We're silent for a moment. Now I knew what had happened to Waldmann. But what about David McLean?

"Was he a spy or wasn't he?"

"I don't know, Rennie. If he was, we didn't know about it. And he never spoke to me about it again."

I remember the notebook pages in code. I have them in my pocket. I pull them out and show them to Ari, but he just shrugs.

"Looks like some kind of code," he says.

"Can you read it?"

He shakes his head.

"So that's it?" I say.

"I'm afraid so." He glances over my shoulder, and a soft smile crosses his face.

Grandma slides back into her chair. A waiter is right behind her with three glasses of champagne on a tray. He distributes them to us.

"The countdown is going to start," Grandma says, raising her glass to a new beginning.

We count backward from ten with everyone else in the place. We all yell, "Happy New Year." Grandma kisses both Ari and me, and I kiss her. Then I get out my phone and text my cousin Adam. Mission accomplished.

Sort of.

The next morning, we meet in the lobby of the Holiday Inn—Grandma and Ari and I.

"I need to make a stop before we leave," I tell Grandma. "I need to return this." It's the photo album I took from Curtis's room.

We stop at the old man's house.

I don't want to get out of the car. I don't want to climb those porch steps and ring the bell. I definitely don't want to talk to the old man. But sometimes you have to do a thing even if you don't want to. So I get out of the car.

Katya answers the doorbell. I tell myself that whatever she decides to say to me, it's okay. She has a right to be angry. But she doesn't yell at me or tell me to get lost. And when I tell her that I want to talk to her grandfather, she steps aside to let me in. I glance over my shoulder to Ari's car and see my grandmother. She nods her encouragement: *You can do this, Rennie.*

Gerry is in the living room, his feet on the coffee table. He's in the same clothes he was in last night when he came to the police station to get Katya. He looks blearily at me but doesn't say a word.

Katya leads me down the hall to the old man's room. Before she knocks on his door, she says, "The police found someone for me to talk to—about the safe-deposit box, I mean. I'm not sure what's in it. I only know what Noah told me. But if it is what he told me, these people can help me track down any relatives so their valuables can be returned. For things where there is no one, they say I can give it to a good cause. I was thinking maybe a Holocaust museum or a memorial."

She doesn't wait for me to say anything before she knocks on the door. Inside, the old man grunts. Katya pushes open the door.

"You have company, Grandpa."

Curtis is slumped in a chair beside his bed. He looks smaller than the last time I saw him. Older and grayer too. He peers at me through glazed eyes. I glance at Katya.

"I don't think he slept well last night," she says. "I don't think any of us did. Because of Eric. Maybe I'm stupid or naïve—or both—but I didn't think he had anything to do with those college kids. I guess I didn't want to believe it. I'm sorry for what he did to you." She raises a hand, and for a moment I think she's going to touch the bruise on my face. "I'm sorry for what Noah did too."

She slips away, leaving me in the doorway. I hold out the small leather photo album.

"I borrowed this. I wanted to return it before I go back home."

I take it to him. He doesn't move. I put it on the bed. He still doesn't move. I have no idea what to say. What comes out is, "I'm sorry I broke in here. I just had to know."

"I hated him." His voice is raspy. "He was a cruel man. He did terrible things, and I hated him."

What can I say to that? I look at all the stuff crammed into his room: the medals, the uniforms, the flags, the books.

"I was looking for answers," he says, following my eyes. "I thought I could figure out what made him do what he did. But none of it helped. It doesn't explain anything."

"I'm sorry," I say. It's time to leave, but I hesitate. "My grandma…she saw a picture in there of you and Mirella. She thinks you were in love with her."

One of his hands seeks out the album and settles on top of it.

"She never should have married him. Her parents talked her into it. They thought he would provide for her. And when she heard we were going to America—she was so happy."

"Well, at least she got here."

He looks up at me. "I thought she would be happy too. I thought we both would."

It takes a few seconds before I absorb that word. *Both*. Not all. Both.

"Everything was upside down after the war, not just in Europe, but everywhere. Even in Buenos Aires. There were foreigners everywhere. The Cold War was heating up. People were selling information. Everyone was trying to make money. There were people who knew people, people with connections. So when your grandfather arrived and my father announced that the Americans wanted him, that he was going to work on new weapons for their military…" His hand closes around the small album. "I whispered a few words in an ear. It didn't take long. Someone approached me."

He'd told me my grandfather was responsible for what had happened to his father. But that was true only in an indirect way. Curtis was the one who had tipped off the Russians to where Waldmann was. Maybe he wouldn't have done it if David McLean had never been sent to Buenos Aires. But Curtis, not my grandfather, was the one who'd sealed Waldmann's fate.

"My father arranged to send all our possessions on ahead of him, with me and Mirella to take care of everything, like a pair of servants. He was supposed to join us in California after the Americans had debriefed him. But he never showed up." A tiny smile flickers across his face.

"And Mirella?"

"When she found out who my father really was, she left. I went after her, but she refused to see me or talk to me. I lost track of her until she showed up in town looking for work. I was already married."

He picks up the album and hands it to me. "Take it," he says. "I don't want it anymore."

"But—"

He thrusts it at me. I have no choice. I take it.

He's staring out into space. It's like he's forgotten I'm in the room. What can I do? I leave, closing the door behind me. Katya is in the front hall. I give her the album. "In case he wants it sometime," I say. "Or for you to keep. It belongs here."

She takes it but doesn't open it. I can't tell if she's ever seen it before.

She opens the door for me, and I step out into the crisp sunshine of a new day and a new year. Ari gets out and opens the rear door for me. Grandma reaches back over the seat and squeezes my hand.

"Do you have your passport, Rennie?" she asks.

I nod. Carver returned it and my driver's license. They're both in my back pocket. I've got my duffel too. We had swung by Jacques's place to get it.

As Ari pulls away from the curb, I think about Katya and her fears. Then I think about my grandfather, about David McLean and how little I know about him, about how little his own daughters probably know about him. My grandmother is looking straight ahead. I wonder how much she knew. But mostly, I wonder how much of me comes from him. Like Katya, I wonder what part of me comes from the dead.

ACKNOWLEDGMENTS

A heartfelt thank-you to Eric Walters, Ted Staunton, Richard Scrimger, Sigmund Brouwer, Shane Peacock and John Wilson—gentlemen all—who cooked up the idea of a sequel in my absence. A big thanks to Andrew Wooldridge for going along with the idea. And to Sarah Harvey—thank you for being so sane and sensible.

NORAH McCLINTOCK writes mystery and crime fiction for young adult readers. She is the author of the Chloe and Levesque, Mike and Riel, Robyn Hunter, and Ryan Dooley series, as well as many stand-alone novels. Norah grew up in Montreal, Quebec, is a graduate of McGill University (in history, of all things) and lives in Toronto, Ontario. She is a five-time winner of the Crime Writers of Canada's Arthur Ellis Award for Best Juvenile Crime Novel. Her novels have been translated into sixteen languages. Visit www.norahmcclintock.com for more information. *From the Dead* is the sequel to *Close to the Heel*, Norah's novel in Seven (the series).

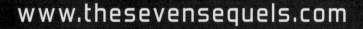